I0682875

Soul-Augmented Part 2

Kas Smith

Copyright © 2016 Kevin Self
Produced by Sci-fi Visionaries
All rights reserved.
ISBN: 978-0-9954561-6-7

DEDICATION

To those who have suffered a loss

CONTENTS

WELCOME TO YOUR GCD

Download the Sci-fi Visionaries app from the Apple or Google Play store to transform your device into your very own Genius Control Device (also known as GCD). Your GCD will assist you to deliver an enhanced experience. Wherever you see a Layered Vision symbol on the left-hand side of the page of the novel, please scan the symbol (also called markers) and content will appear in augmented reality. Tap the text or image, then pinch them to increase or decrease their size. If more than one marker appears on the page, move the GCD off of the page, then back to the new marker to view the content.

Please note: the app is not needed to enjoy this novel, it is just an added bonus.

Try scanning this marker

CHAPTER ONE

FATAL ERROR They all crept backward. Shock locked their jaws. In all of Joshua and his team's research and theoretical notations—they never saw this coming.

The worm went from violently wiggling to constantly flipping over, to sliding around in a frantic circle.

'Billy!' Van DeMay called out. 'What's wrong with him?'

'I think it's going insane,' Jonahs said.

'No,' Joshua replied sharply. 'This is worse. Much worse.'

'Why?' Zahurska asked, hyperventilating in response to his words.

'Because it's mutating.'

His statement became obvious when, to their astonishment, the creature's size expanded before their eyes and it burst out of the glass dish. Joshua wondered if its growth hormones had been triggered as he witnessed the worm's mass ten-folding. It's thorny bristles transformed into crab-like legs, ripping through its reddish-gray body with a wretched tearing of flesh. Within seconds it became the size of a large dog.

'I'm raising the alarm,' Zahurska cried. She was quick to make good on her words.

The writhing grotesque mass of the animal released a loud echoing shriek until all life within seemed to stop and it curled up like a dead bug. They ventured closer, Jonahs leading the group. A putrid scent emanated from the critter; the smell of days-old,

1

necrotic flesh.

Instantly the worm reanimated and began scurrying around, shrieking from the torturous pain of its own accelerated growth.

'We can't let it get away,' Joshua said. He contemplated that with energy and mass being related, with the amount of energy that had been pumped into the creature, its mass could soon become far greater.

'I'm getting out of here,' Van DeMay said, dropping the sensor probe he held and backing away.

It took moments for the worm to grow as large as an adult man. It took even less time for the rest of the group to follow Van DeMay's lead. It lunged at the fleeing Dr. Pierre with an ear-rupturing shrill, crashing through a table and breaking electronic glass beakers. The mass of the abomination fell upon the hapless victim, and to their utter horror they saw the creature's body sucking the man into it as he screamed. It was a sound of suffering Joshua had never heard. Joshua grabbed Pierre's only free hand.

'I've got you,' Joshua said as Pierre screamed for help.

Zahurska came to both their aid, grabbing her colleague's arm. Joshua exhausted his full strength trying to pull Pierre free, but the worm's gross segmented, tubular mass absorbed the mathematician like quicksand.

'Get back!' yelled a security personnel upon entering the Quantum Room.

Joshua was slow to oblige, and Zahurska had to yank him away as the guard's handgun rounds swallowed by the body of the ever-growing creature; each shot further angering the monstrosity and drawing its attention. Its body split open, revealing a heinous circular row of triangular teeth. Moving backwards in dread, the guard was pounced upon. Joshua covered his eyes to limit the revolting view of the man being swallowed head-first—his legs severed. Panic rung out in the chamber. Hannerman and Mr. Moreau emerged from the airlock to witness the gruesome attack; behind them were members of Ghost Team One, armed with their advance weapons.

'Holy shit!' Wingman said, his eyes trying to adjust to the chaos. 'What the fuck are you people doing in here?'

Peacemaker and Tombstone pushed ahead of him to behold the scene.

'Kill that thing,' Moreau ordered.

Hannerman shouted for them to wait. 'Do not use your KEP rifles.' He was fully aware of the penetrability of the rounds they used on the neo-humans. 'You might damage the Quantum Transcender or the power cells.'

Peacemaker dashed forward barging Wingman out of his path and raising his rifle to fire. 'Out of my fucking line of sight, sir,' he said to Hannerman—not interested in protecting the all-important machine. He raised his weapon, but a dark hand shoved it back into his chest.

'You'll blow us sky-high if you hit the battery strings,' Black Knight said, face to face with him.

'We're already sky-high, fucker.'

'Use small arms only,' Tombstone commanded the team. 'Secure the chamber.'

The rest of the team pulled out their handguns and unleashed short bursts of shots as they circled out of the creature's way. Joshua stood protectively in front of Zahurska—forced to endure more of the worm's loud shrieks; it was worse than a distressed pig's squeal. The worm crashed through data storage racks before it became immobilized and lifeless. Ghost Team One closed in on the stench left by the mutated worm. Though motionless, its skin sizzled, shifting its form as though being pulled and twisted from the inside. Its elongated, newly grown limbs rhythmically twitched.

Loca swore, making sure to keep in close proximity to The Boogieman. At six foot eleven and near four hundred pounds, he would have given the beast a run for its money.

'Hold your fire,' Tombstone ordered, finally convinced the creature's lifelessness was irreversible.

While the rest seized, Black Knight continued to pump it full of bullets, ripping chunks of the creature's guts over the glass floor. Its blood sprayed all over the broken computer systems and his combat armor. He finally released the trigger. At the same time, Peacemaker pulled out his cutlass and began hacking away at the already dead monster's flesh with unexplainable anger. Being drenched in its putrid blood mattered little to him.

'I'm sure it's dead now, Lance Corporal,' Tombstone said.

'Status report Ghost team,' Colonel Marcs said. His voice could be heard by all from the room's intercommunication system. 'Tell me that room is secure, over.'

'That's affirmative, Colonel,' Tombstone said in his personal comms link. 'Assessing casualties now, sir.'

'Idiot!' Moreau said, looking at Joshua. 'You could have destroyed decades of work.'

'Two people are dead, is that all you care about?' Joshua said. The shock of the ordeal still hadn't fully dissipated from his shaky fingertips. He held Zahurska in his arms trying to contain the effects of the traumatic experience, while her tears dampened his shirt. Van DeMay held his head with both hands in disbelief. Jonahs simply stood, his hands on his hips, emotionless as he stared at what looked like remains of human bodies covered in pink and white puss-like worm guts. Joshua saw how Jonahs watched Peacemaker slash away at the worm and didn't even break a sweat.

'Their lives are on your head,' Moreau said. His R-MEN guardians had returned to his side.

'That's enough soldier!' Tombstone said to Peacemaker.

Finally, he desisted his assault after a few more downward stabs at the carcass. Joshua winced at the actions of the special ops operator. He had a sadistic look in his glare as he tried to regain his breath. Peacemaker wiped the broad blade with his pants leg, serving no purpose since his clothes had just as much blood on it.

'You've got some issues man,' Wingman said, raising his tattooed eyebrow. 'I don't know who touched you when you were a child.'

The Boogieman, who wore a vest revealing swollen, sculpted biceps, shook his head at the sight. While Loca covered her nose from the unbearable stench.

Peacemaker got back up from his knees, his blood still racing. Panting, he took hefty strides up towards Black Knight and squared up to him. 'I'm surprised you didn't want to hang back and send someone else to die.' He raised the cutlass to the taller man's face, but Black Knight didn't flinch. 'What happened to you homeboy? You used to enjoy killing.'

Peacemaker wiped the blood-stained blade on Black Knight's shoulder and the black soldier grabbed his hand with a vice-like grip so strong the psychotic soldier gritted his teeth to hold back the pain that surged through him. He unwillingly dropped his blade as the tendons in his wrist squeezed close to breaking point.

'Stand down, both of you,' Moreau ordered. 'Before I throw both your asses in the brig.'

One of the robots analyzed the soldier's delayed tension and stepped forward. 'Please desist from your hostilities, violence is unnecessary.'

The humanoid machine spoke with the gentleness of tone, as though clemency and kindness were at the core of its programming. Black Knight motioned jointed into action like he had heard startling bang and immediately he released his iron grip.

'Get the fuck away from me,' he said reaching for his weapon.

It was clear to Joshua that the usually dispassionate soldier, who hadn't flinched at the sight of the giant worm nor teammate's madness, now had lost his cool.

Peacemaker picked up his cutlass, smiling all the while. He then wagged his blade like it was his index finger. 'It's a shame we can't kill every monster. The real ones come back for you.'

'Dr. Hannerman,' Moreau said. 'We better get a detail to survey for any hull fractures and get someone to clean this mess up.'

'What happened, Joshua?' Hannerman said, coming to his side.

'It worked for the tree trunk. I was certain I compensated for the differences in the worm's cellular structure in the biological mapping; the plastids, the Vacuole, the lack of Chloroplast. But I must have overlooked how much more geometrically complex biological life is on the quantum level. I can correct it, it will just take a bit more time.'

'Dr. Smith,' said Colonel Marcs' voice. 'From now on, I'm going to be posting armed personnel inside the Quantum Room while you work.'

CHAPTER TWO

HE KNOWS WHAT MUST BE DONE

The sadness and sense of frustration and failure lingered in Joshua's mind after the incident. Despite Dr. Pierre being a shy and mostly quiet presence, he was adored by all in the team. They dedicated a short amount away from their work to share a few words and fond memories they each had of him—except for Jonahs. Silence was the only symptom of his bereavement, if he grieved at all. Dr. Zahurska, whose tear-filled eyes showed how much she was affected by his death, revealed that Pierre was actually one of the Circle of Hermes' most respected scientist. He had made his name, not in the field of science, but finance. His mathematical prowess was instrumental in the rise of suron coin and he was an architect in the demise of state currencies. It was Moreau who realized that Pierre's skills could best be utilized on project Reclamation Olympus.

Joshua was surprised at how quickly his remorse faded as he insisted they resumed their work. He convinced himself that it was his desire to save Savannah that had overridden all other sentimentality. But a notion had begun to take hold in his mind, *"Is this what dire circumstances do to men of ethics? Degrade one's morality and empathy? Am I now losing my humanity like all the others?"* He shrugged off the distracting emotions and decided to soldier on; tunnel vision had always been one of his dominant characteristics.

As he worked on, armed teams continuously monitored from a

distance, taking shifts. Yet he noticed that Black Knight hardly ever left. His other Ghost Team members chatted amongst themselves, paying little interest in Joshua's work. But the tall, dark-skinned soldier would pace the chamber, inspecting ever piece of machinery, his particular interest was the teleportation machine. When Joshua caught his eye, Black Knight would stare back, never breaking eye contact and his eyes would react by narrowing, like a predator tracking its prey. After a while, the team of scientists did their best to ignore him—there was just something too creepy about the man and looking at him made it worse. So much so, that Dr. Zahurska asked if Joshua could request that the soldier be removed from his detail. Joshua preferred not to do anything that would agitate the man, fearing his mysterious nature.

The intense testing continued, and after multiple iterations of alterations the teleported worms no longer mutated. Though they died in every instance, fully intact. The never-ending experiments took its toll on all the scientists, but Joshua's determination to come up with new ideas and solutions never wavered. That didn't stop Hannerman's increasing concerns about Joshua's lack of sustenance and the overall deterioration in the appearance of the once handsome man. The determined physicist would take short naps, but be woken up by either new ideas or nightmares of Savannah.

'So close, but yet so far,' Joshua said to himself. He hunched over in a rotating chair staring endlessly at the computer screen's simulation of the quantum world. He had hit a low point, all the energy he had left was channeled into watching the purple and red particles on the display, and how they appeared and disappeared.

'Another round of coffee?' Zahurska came over his shoulder with a steaming cup of his usual black, no sugar.

'You read my mind. Thank you.' He had smelt her coming. The jasmine and rose fragrance were quite unlike Savannah's, but still alluring.

Jonahs was slumped over his desk out cold. Van DeMay was sipping his coffee, still disoriented from the breaking of his slumber.

'You know,' Zahurska said, flicking her fingers to ease the burn of the cup, 'a good night's sleep would be more effective than caffeine.'

'I can't sleep,' Joshua said, his resolution hung in his weary voice. 'I just can't figure out why the specimens keep dying. It's almost like...'

'Like what?'

'We can teleport an inanimate object and life as basic as multicellular lifeforms like plants. Complex life may share all of the subatomic elements and many of the same base elements, like carbon, hydrogen, nitrogen. But the complexities go far beyond base elements. Perhaps we could succeed, ten years from now, five maybe.'

'Look how far we've come. It won't be long now. You've been an inspiration to all of us. We'll keep working with you to solve this.'

He needed her assurance. He stared at her and being up close, he felt a certain discomfort for the first time. He was an expert at quantum mechanics, not male-female social dynamics. But Zahurska's beauty was striking, and he saw the glow in her blue eyes. 'How did a girl like you get caught up in the Circle of Hermes?'

'Well, that's a long story. I don't get involved in any toppling of regimes or installing new world orders and stuff like that. I'm just a biophysicist.'

'Yeah, but they're murderers.' He couldn't help letting his animosity dictate his choice of words.

She paused at first. 'Ternopil Oblast, ever heard of it?'

Joshua shook his head.

'I doubt you would have. If there's a place on Earth poorer and more overcrowded, I wouldn't want to know about it either. It's where my family's from. It used to be beautiful. Nothing grows there anymore. There's no natural life. Outside of Tokyo and LA, it has the most layered vision aforms in any metropolitan area. Almost every tree you see, every bird chirping as it flies above your head—isn't real. Cockroaches make up the standard diet. They boil them, fry them, roast them. They,' Zahurska stuttered on her words for the first time, trying to find the right ones, 'they helped us, took us out of there. Put me through school.'

'Out of the goodness of their hearts?'

'We're all here by necessity, Joshua. The world we live in, choice... was a luxury; now it's an illusion. It's sad to say this, but I feel that I've seen more bad than good in this world. Perhaps if mankind started again, away from all their conflictions, we could build a better world. From what I heard—we had.'

He reached out, placing his hand on hers. 'You need to leave this place, while you still can. Only evil exists here.' He partly wondered if it was too late for her—that her mind, as well as her body, was trapped in the Circle's web. But he had always sensed a goodness in her heart.

She forced into place an awkward smile, her eyes becoming glazed over. 'We will get there eventually.' The red and purple light of the particles illuminated her features as she bit her lip. She turned, drawn to the computer model just as Joshua was. 'As Einstein said, the quantum world is strange and spooky.'

Joshua craned his neck and squinted at the model. Her words, "the quantum world" forged a thought in his mind, one that he had never conceived in all his years of toil. He touched the display screen repeatedly, exhaling *arrghs* when it refused to function to his gesture command, followed by unintelligible words of frustration.

'You need to flick your wrist properly,' Zahurska said.

'That's what I'm doing.'

She intervened, executing the hand gesture, and in one take, she had pulled the quantum simulation out into the air.

Like a spell being cast, the sight of the hovering AR model enlarged in all its splendor had bewitched him.

'Is everything alright, Joshua?'

She had started to call him by his first name when only few people were in earshot. He pretended not to notice but being in an orbital space station in the under-belly of a powerful secret society and surrounded by hostile strangers, hearing his first name did make him feel more at ease.

'I won't find the answer that I need here. The answer lies in there.'

'In where?'

'The Quantum world. I need to get inside of it.' Joshua rose from his swivel chair.

Van DeMay emerged from his desk to share a glance with Zahurska. 'Err… you want to go inside the computer simulation? Psychiatry is not my specialty, Dr. Smith, but errr…'

'The Reality Room. Take me to it. You must have one.' His sleep deprivation had caused his voice to lose its vigor and passion. But it was revived in his request.

'The ring has one, but access is highly restricted,' Zahurska said.

'If the Circle wants to get to Olympus, I need access to that room.'

'I'll see that it's done,' said an accented voice from the other side of the room.

They all turned and saw Tombstone, next to him stood Black Knight.

'Follow me!' Tombstone said.

***

They made their way along a black corridor that stretched a considerable distance; further than any part of the extraterrestrial facility Joshua had visited. A section of glass spanned its entire length, providing him with a glimpse of Earth, which, despite the anarchy on its surface, spun peacefully from high above.

Tombstone and Black Knight led the scientists, all except Jonahs, who they left asleep. Joshua's feeling was that his Ivy League counterpart's pessimism meant that he would have most likely tried to derail his plans.

The temperature felt colder than the other areas of the Ring, decreasing further the closer they got to their destination. The solar radiation would have heated one side of the station to a sweltering hundred and twenty degrees Celsius. While the shaded side would be minus hundred degrees Celsius, quite a swing for the environmental controls to handle.

Joshua only had the privilege of being within a Reality Room a few times while conducting experiments in an Oxford research center. They were mostly featured inside prominent buildings, wealthy corporations and the homes of the well-to-do. Decked out with an array of sensors, actuators and robotic technology, they could create a fully virtual environment. The rich spent a fortune in there, living out their wildest dreams within virtually constructed worlds; some went broke, unable to unhook themselves from its euphoric effects. They were even equipped with embedded digital scent technology that could make you feel like you were walking through the aroma-intense avenues of Manhattan, replicating the scent of the grilled and roasted street food.

'Sergeant,' Black Knight said, lowering his voice to avoid being overheard, 'this is a bad call.'

'Maybe, but we need results and fast.'

'Moreau will not approve,' Black Knight said. His displeasure was obvious.

'It's our blood that spills every day so that the Circle of Hermes can rule... not Moreau's.'

'Mr. Tombstone,' Joshua said, catching up to the soldier's faster pace. 'Thank you for your help.'

'No problem. I know what it's like to risk it all for those you love,' Tombstone replied. 'The price can be high, sometimes too high.'

It was the first ounce of compassion Joshua had witnessed from the soldier. A surprise from a man whose chest protruded out with pride at all times.

'What was *your* price, Sergeant?' Joshua asked, seizing the moment to discover the nature of such deep words.

'My wife and son were killed by a monster,' Tombstone conveyed with little emotion. He passed his hand across the roughness of his large facial scars as though it was soothing for him.

'What about your scars?' Joshua asked. 'Were they from neo-humans?'

The board man shook his head. 'Religious fanatics! Long story... and a painful one.'

They made it to the double doors of the VR facility, guarded by four R-MEN. For Joshua, it was a startling scene, seeing an RM-V9 series robot gripping a submachine gun. He was still horrified by the video clips of their robotic insurrection. One footage had been permanently etched into his mind, when one of the humanoids had broadcast a message and said that they were now a cybernetic race; who knows what would have happened if they were never stopped. The Circle broken every charter law placing weapons in the hands of RM-V9s. Of all the places on the Ring, Joshua wondered why they chose to do so here.

'Step aside,' Black Knight informed them, with minimal courtesy. 'Our access to the Reality Room has been approved.'

'Unfortunately,' said one of them, 'Ghost Team operator designation: Black Knight, it is currently occupied. Apologies!'

'Stand down, RM-V9s,' Tombstone commanded, and he grimaced. If the likelihood of danger could elicit a fear response in the robot's machine learning algorithms, the Sergeant's tone would have done the trick. His command seemed to have an effect, as the robots remained mute while processing the situation.

A middle-aged woman wearing white robes materialized before them, causing a muttered *what the hell* to depart Joshua's lips. But the oddity of the female aform was lost on both Black Knight and Tombstone and they squared themselves up to the woman.

'Reality Room—open,' Tombstone said to her. 'Please.' He had to pause to build up to the unfamiliar adverb.

'Access denied,' the woman replied, smiling warmly. 'Tombstone.' Her perched owl gave a lazy flapped its wings, turning its head to inhuman angles.

'Please,' said Dr. Zahurska' gentle voice. 'Allow me.' She edged forward with small steps and the men parted for her.

Zahurska said something in a language Joshua could not understand. At first, he thought it was Ukrainian or Russian. But it bared striking resemblance to the unusual language Moreau had spoken before.

'Authorization confirmed, Kateryna,' the old woman replied. 'However, only one of you may enter, until the current occupant gives further approval.' Both the woman and the owl's head turned to one within the group. 'Joshua, why don't you go inside.'

He was taken back by her warm and motherly tone.

The woman vanished, and the R-MEN parted to the side. The solid, wide doors slid open to reveal a bright scene of green and blue. Joshua had thought to question who the mysterious aberration was and why Zahurska had clearance that the Ghost Teams hadn't. Perhaps the science team had a higher level of authorization.

'Dr. Smith,' Van DeMay called out his name. The short man lowered his voice, looking on at the room with awe. 'Zahurska and I will head to the rooms' external control area and set up your simulation from there.'

'Sure,' Joshua replied. He stepped inside with trepidation. Each time his feet applied pressure to the floor, a perimeter of light enveloped his soles, and he could feel the force of the ground pushing back on him, responding to his presence. Glancing behind, he saw Black Knight at the edge of the room.

Being aboard an orbital facility, it took a moment for him to realize he had walked into a VR construct of a beach. His eyes had to adjust to the blazing light of the artificial sun beating upon his cheeks. As they finally did, he made out a silhouette of something in front of him. His vision sharpened and retuned his contrast, color and depth perception. It was a man sitting ahead of him, with his legs folded, gazing out on the abundance of the clearest blue sea. Joshua quickly identified the man as he stepped closer, his shoes sinking into the sand. It was Moreau; the pale crown of his head practically glowed in the simulated sunlight.

The eerie man rocked gently to the sounds of the undulating ocean waves, sheltering underneath the leaves of a coconut tree which bowed at an almost diagonal angle. Joshua heard what sounded like a roar. He saw an animal pouncing towards Moreau, a wildcat, with wide-set yellow eyes that glowed as it moved in for the kill.

'Moreau, look out!'

The older man never flinched, like he couldn't hear Joshua's cries. The big cat approached Moreau and encircled, taming itself with each revolution before settling down next to his side like a friendly house cat.

'This is the only place I can be alone,' Moreau said, his eyes cast into the horizon. 'My guards do not bother me while I am in here. Yet you disturb my restless soul, Dr. Smith.'

'When I heard the puma roar, I thought... instinctively I thought you were in danger.' Joshua stood at the left side of the man, keeping his distance from the puma resting at Moreau's right. It was spooky dealing with the emotions of being close to wild, dangerous animals, even if it wasn't real; Joshua assumed that it wasn't. The cat noticed his presence and flared its teeth at him, wanting to pounce if not for Moreau's caring shushes and commands to be at ease.

'You said you heard it roar. Pumas cannot roar, Dr. Smith. They purr. Cats that purr cannot roar.' Moreau still had yet to look at him.

'Yet, it did roar.'

Moreau's soaked face finally turned to him in its paleness. 'Yet... it did. It is beguilingly strange, to be confined yet feel so free.'

'Wait, when you mentioned your guards, I thought they were for your personal safety?'

'In a way, they are.'

The pale man revealed little details, but Joshua had now built up an image in his mind that the guards served a higher master, and that Moreau was a threat to them as much as an asset. The R-MEN were programmed to watch him.

The leaves of the slanted coconut tree swayed in a gentle breeze, one that he too felt on his cheek. He looked downwards and saw sand grains had covered the edge of his shoes.

'I believe I can solve the matter teleportation puzzle. The answer lies in here.'

'You'll find more than answers in here young lad, things you may not wish to find.'

'I know about Reality Room technology. The most advance ones can tap into your hippocampus to access your memories, they can scan your brainwaves to interpret concepts that lay deep within one's own mind in order to create a richer experience. The answer is already in my mind, I just need help to visualize it.'

'It can do so much more than that. I have disabled the room's monitoring system so that we can have a little chat. You know, once, long ago, I was much like you; young, ambitious, ostentatious... I also lived in London.'

'Were you black as well?'

Moreau turned robotically to him with the sternest of faces. 'Fortunately, no—'

Joshua shouldn't have been surprised by Moreau's annoyance to his cynical question, and yet he was.

Moreau continued. '... given the state of racial injustices in those... unsophisticated times. I was, however, a doctor—a physiologist.'

LAYERED VISION

Behavioral Sink

'You prefer to not use the title?' Joshua said, recalling never hearing him being referred to as a doctor.

'The title used me, magnifying my desires to points of no return. Like you, I wanted to use my talents to change the world. I foresaw this… behavioral sink that society has found itself in—overpopulation, murders, moral decay, racial contamination of the gene pool.'

'Okay!' Joshua stressed each syllable of the word. 'I don't think we're anything alike.'

Moreau's raised an eyebrow. 'No? Not even in our desire, for a child to never lose their parents to monsters that prey on the weak.'

The words flared Joshua's rage. 'You sir, are malevolent.'

'Perhaps, perhaps. But I was not always. One can become that which they despise far easier than one would believe possible—as you may know. My aspiration was to rescue man from an ill fate, so we can be better.' Moreau released coughs from the depths of his lungs that would make anyone's throat sore. He soon resettled, but a look of distress lingered with him.

'Are you sick or something?'

The puma seemed to sense the old man's condition and began to rub its head on him and lick his face.

'Yes, this is the only place that soothes my pain outside of a med-tank and without Andro-opioids. I am dying from something that cannot be cured; which corrupts my mind and my body. That is why I want you to succeed, Dr. Smith.'

Moreau's wet checks smiled as his sweat melted into the almost white sand. It was then that Joshua noticed that there were indentations in the sand right next to Moreau, like someone was sitting previously on the other side of him.

'Was someone here with you?'

'Yes. The lady whom you saw. But that is all I wish to say on that matter.'

Joshua knew there was no point giving into his intrigue to know more based on the way had Moreau shut down the matter. "So, that's your aim? To live forever as a neo-human?'

'Death is feared by many in this world—except those who have truly witnessed its beauty of simplicity. Immortality is the lust of the Circle and their adversaries, the Builders of Jericho. But I have seen enough… of life, and I believe our mortality is a part of the human condition, helping to identify and define who we are. The laws of identity states that an entity without an identity would cease to exist. So, without our mortality, mankind too will cease existing.'

'If you don't want the same thing as the Circle, what is that you want?'

'I merely desire to keep what I have worked so hard to create; for my mind to not degenerate and become what I have spent my life trying to cure. If the Circle will not allow me to die as man, then I prefer to live... beyond men. We may not have started off on the right foot, but we do want the same thing, which is for you to succeed. Olympus offers us both a fresh start. You will have as much time within the Reality Room as you require. Succeed, and you will bathe in suron coin, enough to buy your own town in a subterranean city. Or to give your wife the exowomb she undesired.'

Moreau's last statement made Joshua's eyes narrow. For him to mention the artificial womb meant that he had been paying more attention to him than Moreau had conveyed.

'More power than you can ever imagine,' Moreau continued. 'The power to change the world as you see fit. As I had attempted so long ago. Tell me, what would you do with such power?'

The question threw the young physicist off guard. He shrugged his shoulders. 'I wouldn't want it, because I'd probably mess things up. Power belongs...in better hands.'

Moreau neither responded nor reacted to Joshua's answer. Then, with an awkward balance, he rose up and calmly readjusted his outfit before replying. 'Good luck Dr. Smith. Where you dare to tread, you will need it.' The chest display in his suit cycled through his vital signs status updates. 'Reality Room – reactivate monitoring and end simulation.' The room transformed in a flash into an empty area with smooth blue walls and spotlights of a brilliant white covered the floors, walls and ceiling in rows.

'So confined, yet so free,' Moreau said.

He walked away and Joshua watched as he exited, more puzzled by the man than ever before.

'Dr. Smith, can you hear us now?' said Van DeMay's voice over the room's speakers.

Instinctively Joshua looked around, but realized it was not possible to see anything outside the room, with the exception of the open entrance. 'Yes, I can,' he said, eager to get going. 'Please start the simulation.'

'Smith!' Black Knight called out from the doorway. His eyes glanced to the side and then to the ceiling of the room as he balanced on the entrance's edge. Despite Moreau's personnel restrictions being lifted, the soldier was obviously fearful to step inside. 'If I were you, I would not stay within these walls for long. One can lose sense of what is reality.' His message conveyed concern for Joshua's wellbeing, but his piercing eyes felt similar to a lion waiting amongst the tall grass for its moment to kill, having to calm itself until the chance arose.

The door closed.

'Joshua,' Zahurska called out over the speakers. 'We're uploading the quantum simulation. Should be ready any moment now. We've never really done this before.'

He felt a cold shiver through his spine that lingered far longer than he expected or wanted. His body was trying to tell him something his mind needed to ignore—if he was to succeed.

'Upload complete,' Van DeMay said. 'I'm about to run the simulation now, Dr. Smith.'

In an instant, blinding hues of primary colors assaulted his vision. Joshua closed his eyes and still felt the need to shield the abundance of light with his hands.

'Decrease the brightness!' Joshua pleaded.

'Luminosity reduced to sixty-five per cent now, doctor,' Van DeMay said.

Joshua squinted as his eyes reopened to a majestic scene. The room was transformed into clouds of red, blue and green, with cyan, magenta and yellow to a lesser extent. When his vision fully refocused, he could make out individual moving objects. He held his breath for a moment in sheer amazement. Most people dream of seeing picturesque landscapes, bustling foreign cities or ancient ruins, but this was what Joshua had longed to witness, the quantum world.

The quarks, electrons, neutrinos, gluons and photons transverse the space around him; the fastest ones were shaped like peanuts and bagels. The slower the subatomic particles moved, the more the shapes changed to rectangles with semicircles at opposite sides, then to almost perfect spheres.

The ground beneath his feet had changed to blobs of matter and the pressure sensors and actuators on the floor activated to create the sensation that he was stepping on a nonuniform substance.

He couldn't close his mouth. 'A world within a world. A universe in itself.' Joshua spun around to take it all in. 'Ok, now, load the matter teleportation sequence and results into the room. Not my model, the real-life results from our experiments.'

More subatomic particles burst into existence above his right shoulder, making him step back to get out of the way.

'Teleportation data of Worm specimen 312-' Zahurska was annoyed to be interrupted by her short colleague.

'Ted!' Van DeMay said.

'What?'

'His name's Ted.'

'And the other worm's name was Bill?'

'Yeah, but he prefers Billy.'

Zahurska turned away from him shaking her head. 'The teleportation data for 312 has been loaded.'

Joshua watched as more flavors of quarks sprung up before him, Higgs and gauge bosons followed and leptons. He looked down, below him was a three-dimensional vastness, being filled with repetitions of more particles. They popped and crackled as they moved, and the loud bangs of particle-antiparticle annihilations were quickly attenuated by Van DeMay. It was no longer a room, the views stretched out to an infinite distance. He felt like he was standing in a stellar nebula; walking in deep space.

'What exactly are these images we're seeing?' Zahurska asked, she was out of her depth within this quantum world.

'That,' Joshua gave a long pause, 'is our problem, Dr. Zahurska.' He glanced at the lightshow and how it altered before him as more and more groups of particles emerged. An aggregation of attracted charged particles formed an unbroken tube of light and sizzled with excited energy. Clumps of Higgs bosons entered into one side and disappeared. 'That there is the Quantum channel.' Joshua spun three-sixty to take in all of his surroundings. 'Once the object enters the quantum world, many different variations of it is created. The quantum channel cannot decipher what sub-atomized matter is *our* object. They are all our worm.'

'Ahh yes, the many-worlds quantum phenomena,' Zahurska said. 'We should get Jonahs down here.' She knew there was little help either Van DeMay or herself could provide. Her expertise was to assist with the biological-to-molecular component of the quantization process, quantum mechanics was Jonahs' specialty.

'It's alright,' Joshua said. 'You know what? This is going to take a while. Put the simulation on repeat and set the controls to voice activation. You guys go get some rest.'

'I'm not sure that's a good idea, doctor,' Van DeMay said.

'Once I'm done in here, I'll need your minds fresh. Just give me a moment.'

'Ok,' said a concerned Zahurska. 'But we'll be checking up on you periodically. Be careful.'

***

He couldn't tell how much time had passed. The teleportation sequence continued to appear in an endless loop, and Joshua remained spellbound by his unsurpassable problem. He used his GCD to confirm the mathematical calculations he performed in his head. The results were the same as they had analyzed. He eventually gave into his weary legs' urges to sit, and he leaned against the invisible wall of the room, gazing at the moving particles like a fireworks display.

'Hello, Joshua,' a gentle voice said.

Standing at his right side was a woman. She wore a thin cardigan over a flowery summer dress, which swayed gently at its ends when particle and antiparticles annihilated and produced energy.

Intense emotions gripped Joshua's body, forming lumps in his throat. Only the power of time allowed him to break free eventually and speak. 'How are you here?'

'I've always been here.'

His face contorted. 'No, you haven't been; it's been so hard without you. My life's been a mess.'

'It didn't have to be, baby.' Peppered over the woman's cheeks were small, dark bumps; trademark facial moles of the women in his family. Her hair color was another family commonality—a sun-kissed orangey-brown. 'This is your life, why are you ruining it?'

'I've never been the same, since…' He couldn't bear to speak of the tragedy with her standing in front of him. Before long, tears trickled down to his stubble. 'I couldn't cope. All the money I threw into therapy couldn't fix me. I was suicidal, Savannah brought me back from the brink. She saved me, and now, I can't even save her.'

'What does it take to save her?' said the woman. Her mocha skin looked freshly creamed and glistened from the hues of the particles.

'I need to solve a puzzle. An impossible one.'

The simulation was still running, and the intense light of the quantum channel illuminated their bodies. The woman glanced up to view the spectacle.

'That puzzle?'

'Yeah.'

She frowned with a big shrug of her shoulders. 'Why?'

'It's the key to get to her without dying in the process. I couldn't make it to you in time. It feels like fate is repeating itself.'

'No,' her plaited hair swung as she shook her head.

'No? What do you mean?'

'No, why would you try to solve a puzzle if you already know how to solve it?'

'I don't understand.'

'You still don't get it. I've always told you, sometimes, the mind that started with a problem isn't the mind that can solve it. You know what you need to do. I have to go now, son.'

The woman turned to leave.

'Wait!' Joshua's heart catapulted. He jolted forward. 'Don't go, mom. Please!' Impulsively he reached for her with both hands.

The woman shifted backwards, rolling her shoulders away from him. 'Let go!' she cried. Her facial features contorted in anger.

Joshua heard another voice in the room call out, a faint echo barely detectable over the sound of the particles interactions. He turned to his right and to his bewilderment half the Reality Room had transformed into the interior of an apartment. It took him a moment to realize that it was his home, or more precisely, what it would have looked like renovated to a higher standard and minus the extensive cracks and subsidence.

'Mum.' He turned back to find her, but she was gone. The whole room was his home now. But the despair of the woman's disappearance hadn't time to sink in as he glanced at his double-glazed window and an unusual sight caught his eye. Venturing toward the window, he beheld a bright scene of hundreds of apartment units that never existed outside of his London flat. The space between him and the neighboring apartments was a hexagonal shape filled the with residential and commercial cubed units, with a two-hundred meter in diameter void at the center. He leaned over through the open window as far as he could—all he saw were encircling, descending rows of property units that never ended. The view upward was the same, and with that, his suspicion was confirmed.

'An Earthscraper,' he said to himself. He was in one of the underground cities.

Light on surface above shone downward, reflected by mirrors to illuminate interiors space. There was a park where kids climbed trees and raced on their maglev skates. To his left, two levels lower, an exercise-junkie ran a treadmill in a spacious gym with his eight-pack on display. Flash-elevators crisscrossed like the plaid lumberjack shirt, and ferried passengers to their homes, bars and cinemas.

He had never seen so many people smiling, laughing, with no hazard wear in sight. Joshua heard the voice again and unmistakability of its owner my him gasp. He grabbed his chest with splayed fingers.

'Savannah?'

She didn't respond to his call. Her attention lay on the closed bedroom door.

'What's taking you so long?' Savannah said, back still faced him. She wore her highest red heels, that matched her clutch bag as well as her lipstick. The combination stirred his blood as always.

A sigh of relief squeezed every breath from his lungs. 'Baby,' he couldn't get the words out. He reached out both arms to hug her from behind, almost salivating to taste the scent of her perfume when he kissed her neck.

Before he could close the gap, the bedroom door opened. A man rushed out, dapper from head to toe in a gray tailored three-piece. The tall, muscular man groomed like a fitness model grabbed her by her lower back with masculine strength, and leaned toward her with puckered lips.

'Get away from her,' Joshua screamed, launching himself to pull her away.

'No!' Savannah finally addressed him. Her voice could push a charging lion back with its power.

'Don't touch her!' Joshua yelled. 'Who is this? Get out. Get the hell out of here!'

'Josh,' Savannah said sternly, the way he often pushed her to speak to him. She drew out the words slowly for maximum impact. '*Let me go.*'

Defiance forced his head to shake, remembering the horror of her request. They were the exact same words she told him when she ended their relationship outside of the science convention, that ill-fated day. 'I would never. I could never.'

'Let me go.'

She disappeared before him, the stranger and everything in the room followed. Joshua found himself in three hundred and sixty degrees of darkness. He couldn't even see his hand in front of his face as he wept within the void—the black emptiness surrounding him reflected what was within.

Punished by the harshest of images, he dropped to the floor, sitting with his knees elevated and his back to the cold wall. His face slumped into his arms, repeating the word *why* as he cried. His unbreakable resolve had been broken.

Over his head, he heard his name being called by Savannah's sweet voice. Joshua lunged, grabbing hold of her arm with desperate force, neglecting the pain it would have inflicted.

'Let go!'

'No!' he cried, his rational mind needing split seconds to catch up.

Dr. Zahurska stood before him, with Jonahs approaching.

'You're scaring me, Joshua. Are you ok?'

He saw himself gripping her lab coat's sleeve, and then surveyed the Reality Room which resumed back to its default blue. 'I saw her.'

'Who?'

'Savannah. She was here.'

'In the simulation?'

Joshua's eyes kept searching around the room. 'I'm telling you she was in this room. And...'

Zahurska frowned. 'And...'

'And my mother.'

'You told me your mother wasn't here anymore.'

'She isn't, at least not outside of this... reality.'

'That's just crazy,' Van DeMay's said over the speakers. 'I'm fully deactivating the Reality Room. You ignored the safety guidelines and remained in here far longer than permitted. People can suffer from prolonged psychosis as a result of sustained time periods.'

'I think you were dreaming, Joshua,' Zahurska said with a gentle tone.

Joshua shook his head. 'It wasn't a dream.'

'You must have been,' Jonahs said. 'You haven't slept. In here, it would be hard for you to tell the difference. That's why there are strict restrictions on rest periods before entering Reality Rooms.'

'Not even nightmares can be so cruel.' Joshua placed his hands over his face, embarrassed to reveal his pain in front of them. Suddenly, he dropped his arms and jerked forward. 'Wait...' His body froze in suspended animation.

'What is it?' Zahurska asked, kneeling in front of him. 'What's wrong, Joshua?'

'I've found the solution.'

'To matter teleportation?' Zahurska asked.

'Yes. I now know why it had eluded me... because I had already solved the puzzle. I just couldn't see it. We dematerialize matter using energy after infusing it with Higgs bosons. The

LAYERED VISION

Many-Worlds Interpretation (MWI)

bosons encapsulate the then dematerialize quantum energy. We then try to send that energy through a quantum channel that connects two locations together by matching their composition of Higgs particles—their entanglement. The problem is—the process changes the thing that we scan the moment we scan it.'

'Yes, we know all of this,' Jonahs said. 'What's your point?'

'The solution is to not attempt to receive the original matter but accept that once we dematerialize it… it's gone, destroyed. The quantum realm will create all possibilities of the object.'

Jonahs rolled his eyes. 'Yes, Dr. Smith. The many-worlds interpretation, this is academic.' He stressed his statement like he had enough a long time ago.

'We'll search all the of possibilities using the quantum computer and find the quantum iteration that is the same as the original object.'

'Did you fall and hit your head in here?' Jonah said. 'That's over a quadrillion possibilities. There's zero certainty that the reconstituted object will be the same—'

'That's true,' Zahurska said. 'Even if it appeared the same. The difference might be so minute that it would take decades of longitudinal studies to truly be sure.'

'We have to let go of the possibility, and accept that it's gone,' Joshua said.

Jonahs' mouth opened as if to speak, telegraphing a list of responses before finding the right one. 'All this coming from the master of letting go.' His voice raised in pitch and exaggeration.

'Enough Jonahs,' Zahurska said. 'You're a professional. Start acting like one. As our resident expert, do you disagree?'

Jonahs fought with himself to relay his sentiment. 'Yes. But it wouldn't take long to put his theory to the test, so let's see.'

Joshua rose from the floor. 'We just have to believe it will be the same. That it is close enough.'

'Really,' Jonah said as he caressed his pointed chin. 'Just abandon the universal, inviolable laws of physics and mathematics and become believers in faith now?'

Jonahs' contentious remarks had lost their effect on Joshua. Joshua stared at the Reality Room's walls as though his weary eyes were piercing through them and gazing at the stars.

'Whatever faith I had was lost a long time ago, and it's never coming back. But we simply cannot receive what we send. All we have is what the process recreates, and all we can hope for is that our creation is better than Frankenstein's.'

'Alright,' said Jonahs straightening up. 'Let's run some tests. But answer me this; if you're so sure it will work, why do you look so sad? I thought you'd be thrilled?'

'Because he knows it will work,' the voice of Black Knight uttered from afar. He stood at the entrance of the room like it was the edge of a viper pit. 'Sometimes one can only find truth in the depths of tragedy. And a man must let go of what was, so he can become who he must be.'

Joshua sniffled, trying hard to subdue his grief, but the effects on the rooms' virtual constructs was plain to see. He made a solemn walk toward the exit. 'I never want to see this room again.'

CHAPTER THREE

WHAT'S ONE WOMAN'S WORTH

Back within the Quantum Room, they wasted no time putting Joshua's idea to the test. His plan wasn't difficult, or time-consuming to execute; simply radical.

For the first time, Joshua stood back and watched his team prep the experiment. They had repeatedly looked to him for his direction but saw alarmingly that his mind was elsewhere; it had never returned from what it had endured in the Reality Room. Jonahs initiated testing. All except Joshua eagerly look on as a worm specimen was teleported alive and completely unaltered from what all their battery of tests could confirm.

They had done it; he had done it. The team of scientists rejoiced. Hannerman was immediately informed and arrived to see the results. After repeating the experiments on more worms and other animals, and measuring the same positive results, they knew it was official. The scientists all congratulated each other with handshakes and hugs. Zahurska gave Joshua a peck on the cheek. Dr. Jonahs acknowledged Joshua's achievements with a stern 'well done' but without the usually accompanying handshake. It was a euphoric moment for everyone. But for Joshua, it was so much more, his life's work, his boyhood dream. He smiled a moment in silence, dwelling on a single thought. It was a quote from Einstein: "The years of anxious searching in the dark, with their intense longing, their intense alternations of confidence and exhaustion and the final emergence into the light—only those who have experienced it can understand it." Now he could understand it.

Hannerman knew what the best reward was for Joshua's diligence. He had secured a communication link to the hospital so Joshua could find out about Savannah's condition. Up until now, he had to rely on messages sent back and forth via Hannerman regarding Savannah as the Circle had a deep distrust for his father due to his religious practices. Had it been any other preacher, they would have been rounded up and placed into internment camps—if they were lucky.

Joshua went back to his room with newfound hope that his deeds had put him one-step closer to getting the only thing that mattered to him back in his undeserved arms. Hannerman had patched the call from the hospital to his Genius Control Device. On his mattress, relieved by a rare moment of privacy, he activated his device with anxious touches. Hoping to see Dr. Panesar and Savannah, instead his GCD projected an AR image of his father sitting at a desk, his face was as emotionally inexpressive as Joshua had grown accustom.

'Where is Dr. Panesar?' he asked the old man.

'The doctor and his associates were rushed off to deal with the emergencies. Since you've been gone, the situation in London has gotten worse. The injured are flooding the hospital's reception, there are a sea of wounded being treated on the car park floor. And the number of Unknowns is mounting up within the Hive.'

'How is she dad? Has there been any change in her condition?' Joshua couldn't register his father's words. Not being able to see her gave fuel to his anxiety.

'She's still sleeping. They told me that GCDs are not allowed to be used inside the Unknown ward so I'm afraid you cannot see her. I have bad news, son. Her life signs are failing rapidly, according to the doctors, she has less than forty-eight hours to live.'

Joshua screamed at the top of his lungs in his mind but said nothing aloud. He rocked back and forth to calm himself, clenching both his hands.

'Her friend, Chichima, is here,' Rev. Smith said. 'As well as my people, we are doing what we do.'

Joshua knew that "my people" meant the worshippers of his secret congregation and "what we do" could only mean praying.

'Please just do whatever you can, I just need a little more time.'

'She's in good hands, my son.'

'Thanks dad.'

'Don't thank me, it was not my hands I was referring to.'

Joshua scowled at his words. 'Well that's all wonderful, but I think I'll rely on Dr. Panesar and his expertise.'

'Why? Because he smiled nicely and told you to trust him?'

'Look, *dad!* I trusted in God's hands once, while you were doing your missionary work in Africa. *The Lord's work* took her away from me. And after that, you never cared about me, your only focus was doing *his* work. You may try to justify the fact you weren't there, but you'll never convince me.'

'I followed my calling, to show people truth and help the needy and the blind. I wanted you to be a part of that, but after your mother died, you refused.'

'So you put God over your own son.'

'Without him, nothing would be possible. I was in the church doing his work. My desire was for you to be with me, but you ran away from home and refused to come back. You abandoned him, and I could never. While we are at home in the body, we are absent from the Lord. For we walk by faith, not by sight.'

Joshua gritted his teeth in a last ditched attempt to hold back his anger. 'Stop it, dad, just cut it out.'

His father waited a while for his son's mood to simmer down. 'Perhaps it's time for us to visit your mother... together. You can add the layered memorial to her gravestone—sift through what images of her should be displayed. It's been too long since we've all been together.'

Joshua laughed.

'Too much time has passed for us to ever have a proper relationship, and I'm not interested. You wanted to be good at what you believed in, and you are, but what you chose wasn't to be a father—it wasn't me. But you know what the worse thing is? The worst thing is for all those years I hated you, I became you, neglecting everything else that mattered for what I believed in the most.'

'It seems as though you have. But the difference is, my calling commanded me to help others, yours called for you to care only for yourself. And even now, is it love or guilt that compels you my son?'

His father's words always had a way of delivering devastating body blows and this time was no exception. Joshua's dark and weary hands covered his face as he spoke. 'I'm tired of this. All I know is, there's no omnipotent being looking over me.' His voice broke. He tried to restrain his swelling tears. 'I'm alone dad, that's how I've been since I was eleven, when mum died, because of your choices. Until I met Sav, and now…I feel all alone again.'

'You're not alone, Joshua. Demons walk amongst you. But do not despair, for angels walk amongst you too my son.'

Without an impulse to say goodbye, his father's image vanished.

LAYERED VISION

Teleological Argument

***

While the rest of the science team took a much-deserved break, Joshua and Hannerman made the final preparations for the full-scale Quantum Transcender's first trial run. Their next objective was simple; to send an earthworm from Earth to Olympus. So far, all animal specimens displayed no negative symptoms of the procedures. But physiology and brain patterns, with their associated behavioral effects, were all they could measure; the effects on the complexities of human thought was more difficult to determine.

Hannerman always believed that Joshua could succeed where he had failed. Now, with their recent breakthroughs, he maintained an ever-persisting smile as he worked with the theoretical physicist to energize the teleportation machine.

Joshua stared at the giant metal ring that levitated in midair at the center of the contraption. As he did so, Hannerman observed him, easily interpreting his sadness as the young man spun and caressed his own ring. The news of Savannah's updated prognosis had rocked him, and his refusal to eat much had taken a toll on his body; he looked like he had aged ten years. His dashing looks had vanished, and his body odor was noticeable to everyone but seemingly himself. Hannerman wondered if he would recognize him if he saw Joshua somewhere else. He knew he needed to do something.

'Joshua, being the son of a holy man, I'm curious, did you at one time believe in a God?'

'Yeah, when I was a kid. I had no choice but to believe in creationism, heaven and hell and what-not. But it's all nonsense. No God's punishing anyone with diabetes or death… a bad diet and a lack of exercise is.'

'So, you're an evolutionist?'

'Aren't we all, mate? We are scientists.'

Hannerman shrugged; he smiled, happy knowing that his ploy had worked. An intellectual debate was one of the few things with the power to tear Joshua away from his ordeal, albeit temporary. 'I'm not aware of science proving the impossibility of higher beings, with capabilities beyond that of man.'

'I mean, it doesn't disprove of fairies either, but I ain't seen any flying around the magical streets of East London.'

'To achieve teleportation we are in effect, manipulating the very fabric life, of existence… and we're only just figuring this out my friend. Couldn't someone who has existed long before us, or is more advanced, do the same… and more?'

Joshua alerted Hannerman that he was firing up the Transcender and a beam of intense light struck the suspended ultrafaron ring with a ferocious concentration of energy. It was a short burst, and then the machine powered down.

'I would have thought you were the Ring's chaplain from the way you're sounding,' Joshua said.

'Hey, behind biology there's chemistry, when you breakdown chemistry you get physics. The physical world can be defined by mathematics. But it is philosophy that underpins it all. I am merely philosophizing.'

'Ok Aristotle, so this is the teleological argument, that life is so complex it had to have been designed.'

'If the force of the Big Bang explosion had been different by one-tenth to the sixtieth power, life would be impossible. Stephen Hawking estimated that if the rate of the universe's expansion one second after the Big Bang had been smaller by even one part in a hundred thousand million million, the universe would have re-collapsed into a hot fireball due to gravitational attraction.'

Joshua raised his hand and waved off Hannerman in dismissal. 'The mere fact that it is enormously improbable that an event occurred… by itself, gives us no reason to think that it occurred by design… as intuitively tempting as it may be.'

'Ah, you're a proponent of the infinite monkey theorem: that a monkey hitting keys at random on a keyboard for an infinite amount of time will almost surely type any given text, such as the complete works of Shakespeare.'

'It's improbable but not untrue.'

'Dr. Joshua Smith, that is untrue, *only untrue*, if you measured across the timeframe of infinity. The universe is thirteen point eight billion years old… not infinitely old.'

'A thousand years ago, man couldn't venture into outer space. Evolution does have it holes but just because we don't fully understand something now, doesn't mean it's untrue.'

'Are you arguing for science here, or religion?'

'I'm arguing that I haven't seen or heard any voices from God proving that he made anything, so my money's not on that bet.'

'Things which are equal to the same thing are equal to each other.'

'Euclid—and he was a mathematician, not a preacher.'

'Indeed, and you believe in math?'

Joshua shrugged his shoulders. 'It generally doesn't lie.'

'So, if you can believe in evolution even though we can't unequivocally prove it, that means, as Euclid's axiom states, that you can't disbelief religion for that very same reason. You're assuming that we're just missing information, but we already have it, my friend. Science proved there *was* a Big Bang, and that therefore means that evolution assumes life evolved from nothing into something, from nonliving matter to living matter, abiogenesis, in some primordial soup. Science has never been able to prove that.'

As Joshua was about to rebut, he happened to glance at the far side of the Quantum Room and saw Black Knight and the female soldier, Loca, talking. He had gotten used to Ghost Team One's presence, but there was something that made him uncomfortable when Black Knight was on duty. It had an effect on his concentration. At times Joshua wasn't aware of his presence, but felt a creepy, uncomfortable sensation, like the Circle of Hermes were beyond men; that they had supernatural energy. It was when the effects were at their most extreme, where he sweated through his shirt and found it awkward to breathe, he would turn to see the Black Knight watching him. The cold soldier made his body heat rise even within an artificially cooled room.

'Frank,' Joshua said quietly. 'Before the worm incident, was Ghost Team One ordered to follow me while I'm on board this facility?'

'Not from what I'm aware of, but as you may have noticed, my authority has its limits. Is there something wrong?'

'I think they've been spying on me all along.'

'The Ghost Teams, overall, are not a threat. Colonel Marcs runs a disciplined unit and Mr. Tombstone keeps his team in check, somewhat. However, off the record,' Hannerman came closed to Joshua so as not to be overheard, disguising his actions to not draw attention. 'If I were you, I'd stay well away from Mr. Black Knight, and as well as Mr. Peacemaker. Mr. Peacemaker is, well-'

'A maniac, psychopath and perhaps paranoid psychotic?' Joshua asked.

'Exactly! The type of unsavory character that fights fearlessly against powerful soul-ravaging creatures, is the type the Circle needs. Being friends with men like him merely requires a high moral ignorance and a poor sense of smell. Though he's easy enough to understand and therefore avoid.' Hannerman bore a token smile as he spoke on Peacemaker, but then quickly it faded. 'Mr. Black Knight, however, is a... complicated man, the type that intrigues you.'

'But-'

'Have you noticed the look in his eyes?'

Joshua knew instantly what he was referring to. The bearded man's jaundiced eyeballs could make a blind man flinch.

'My first doctorate was in psychiatry. I visited maximum security prisons where we were conducting research on how to reform the dangerously criminal minded and criminally insane. That was over thirty years ago, but it was where I saw that same look for the first time, and I would never forget it.'

Hannerman twitched involuntarily, his wrinkled, white face could only look down, locked onto memories he'd hoped would be forever lost. When he resumed speaking, it was as if his mind had left the facility. 'I've been on this Earth a long time and I can tell you two things; one—that's the look of a man who wishes to no longer be alive, and two—his desire is not merely to die, but to die with dark intentions. And with his type, you really hope they get their first wish and never, ever, their second. Gaze into a soul like that, and one can lose themselves.'

At the other side of the chamber, another conversation took place close to the noisy air handling units which circulated cold air to the computer systems and the soul storage banks.

'You sure know how to show a girl a good time, Knight,' Loca said. Her Afro-Latina hair was cane-rowed in intricate patterns at the scalp before forming one big braid that hung at the back. She grew tired of him ignoring her. 'Caballero!'

The tall man was like a statue, his features carved in permanent mold of pain and aggression.

'Negro!' Snapped the caramel-skinned Venezuelan as she elbowed him in his arm. It broke him out of his spell and he finally looked at her. 'Qué te pasa? You think I haven't noticed? You haven't been able to keep your eyes off of el científico—Smith.'

'Because of him, we will all die.'

'Cut this shit out, Caballero! You're starting to seriously creep me out, man, more than normal. Ay mi madre! Between you and that nutjob, Peacemaker—and you men say women are crazy.'

'I have foreseen it.'

'Of course you've seen it, because we're all going to die *someday*. And at the rate the breakthroughs are accelerating it's going to be sooner than we'd like. Trigger is the fourth man we lost in two weeks. He and Peacemaker were amigos from the SEALs. Trigger's death has turned him loco and brother, he's gunning for you.'

'He didn't always despise me. Before the Andro-opioids conquered his mind, we used to be friends.'

'You and that talking scarecrow were friends. What happened?'

He reflected stoically while he paused from answering, standing rigid, as though ordered to attention. 'I was a monster. He hated me… when I stopped being one. I am not concerned about Peacemaker.'

'Well then be concerned about my ass, and forget this *cabroncita*, Smith.'

'And what becomes of us when we die, Loca? Will our souls be abducted like those held captive in those tanks?' He flicked his head toward the storage cylinders filled with blue liquid and flashing purple balls of light. 'Did they even have a choice?' His nostrils flared as the rhythm of his breathing intensified.

'Those SAS boys made you a thinking soldier. Well, the Circle doesn't want us to think, Caballero, we're here to make surons and to send neo-human scum back to wherever it is they came from. If we do our jobs, we might get a premium economy ticket to Olympus.'

'So you want to end up like one of those abominations?'

'What, a neo-human?'

'They are abominations, there's nothing human about them.' His voice elevated.

'Cállate, Negro!' Loca instantly turned to see that the two scientific personnel that maintained the Quantum Room equipment had noticed them arguing. 'You have a problem, cabron?' she said to the men. 'Or do you want one?' She raised her rifle and the startled men moved away. Loca leaned back toward her teammate, who hadn't seemed bothered by the scientists' eavesdropping. 'Mira! Some people might get a kick out of living forever, some pendejo might want to see his side chick again.'

'What about you?' he asked. His eyes seemed to be watery with sadness. 'Is that why you fight for the Circle? For immortality?'

'Muchos gentes mur...,' she composed herself and started again. 'Many people died in the Caracas big quake—including my parents and my kid sister. After I got tired of loading up their layered memorial every fucking day, I would save every crypto-coin I made just to throw it away in Reality Rooms. Talking to VR reconstructions of mi familia created from data harvested by AI algorithms. Talking to ghosts that will never live again. So, shit yeah, it would be nice to see them again.'

'And perhaps you would have... before *they* had carried out their schemes. So why do you fight for them?'

'Who?'

'Our puppeteers.'

'We shouldn't be having this conversation here. Or anywhere. And stop speaking in that way.' He refused to say another word, or to turn his piercing gaze away from her. His intensity burned through her guard. 'I joined the Circle, hoping to find someone,' she revealed. 'And you?'

Loca's relationship with Black Knight had developed enough over the recent months to be able to interpret his micro expressions. His face was like a mountain, perfectly concealing a thunderstorm behind its peaks. But the slight squint of eyes and movement of his dark, thick lips was like soundless lightning flashes illuminating the summits of his composure.

'Redemption,' he uttered.

Loca grabbed the sleeve of his black uniform. Squeezing the fabric as she balled her fist, she looked him right in the eyes, all to let him know how serious she was. 'I like you, but I've got business on Olympus. Don't ever cross the Circle,' she said, shaking her head. 'Because if the orders are to put a bullet in your head... I will pull the trigger.'

He stared back at her, like it was the first time in their conversation she had his full attention. Although it was aggressive, no woman had ever laid a hand on him, not even affectionately. Her contact caused his senses to light up like the layered vision neon lights of New Tokyo. The scars that dissect her eyebrow and recently scarred cuts from battles couldn't prevent her beauty from radiating. For a man whose life had been void of love, for the first time, he dared to conceptualize something other than how to kill what was in front of him as economically as possible.

'Me he equivocado alguna vez?' Black Knight asked her in his deep voice.

Loca was no doubt as thrown off by his question as for the fact that he ignored her less than subtle threat. She pondered a while and released his sleeve. 'Never! You've never been wrong. That's why Tombstone made you second in command. It wasn't for your charm that's for sure.'

'Then trust me. We will die by his hands.'

'Trust you? I hardly know anything about you. I don't even know your name. I can't figure out how you're able to track the monster-men the way you do, or how you know the things you know. After you saved me and he Boogieman in the Manhattan breakthrough, El hombre grande told me about the things you did in the R-MEN wars, how he never saw someone lose that much blood and didn't die. He said his grandmother used to tell stories that were passed down to her about soul eaters—men who were cursed by witches and had to eat the souls of humans to live their lives. That they gained supernatural powers in the process.'

The scars on Black Knight's face contorted as his head twisted back toward her. 'You got all that out of The Boogieman?'

'Yeah, that was the strange thing, it's the most words I ever heard him say.' She looked over at the young physicist who chatted with Dr. Hannerman and struggled to understand why Black Knight had drawn his conclusion. What was it about the skinny scientist that made him such a threat to their lives? 'What are you going to do about him then?'

'I'll wait till the time is right.'

Across the Quantum Room, Joshua and Hannerman were preoccupied as they continued to indulge in their philosophical debates.

'If people were to ever find out what's happening here,' Joshua said as he configured settings on the Transcender's manual control panel, 'I hope history forgives our part in the wrong we're playing.' He had used the word "we", seeing the old neuroscientist and himself as the same; unwitting accomplices to a powerful organization.

'Perhaps in time, history may view us as pioneers, even saviors,' Hannerman replied.

'I seriously doubt that. I get the feeling you don't fully see the wrong in all of this doctor.'

'I am merely postulating as all good men of science do.'

'You do a hell of a lot of postulating.'

Hannerman shrugged his shoulders. 'I'm old, my friend. What else am I going to do up here to pass time? Play video games?' He continued after Joshua's raised eyebrow to suggest it was a fair point. 'They thought Galileo was wrong in his day because he proposed that the Earth was not the center of the universe. Don't you ever question the concepts of what is right and wrong? Do you really believe what you do every day is right? Socrates believed if one knows what they are doing is wrong, they wouldn't do it. This means that it is impossible for a human being to willingly do wrong because their instinct for self-interest prevents them from doing so. So, in a sense, you and I could only be doing what we believe is right.'

Joshua believed deep down that Hannerman didn't really absolve himself from guilt, and he was just merely debating, so he indulged him. 'People do wrong intentionally all the time, Frank. They take drugs, they slash their wrist—'

'Those people are trying to relieve their problems, and those "perceivable" wrong acts, are the means of their release. Socrates' perspective is that choices, right or wrong, serve the ends that the chooser seeks to obtain and not the means through which the ends are realized. So effectively, one commits self-harm because they believe they are doing right.'

'So that would mean all voluntary wrongdoing or bad actions is due to… ignorance,' Joshua said.

'That's what he believed. Our best hope is that we may avoid the condemnation of selling our souls, for the ironic purpose of preserving other souls.'

'Maybe our souls were never meant to be preserved.'

'Have you never lost anyone dear to you? Not Savannah, someone you have no chance of seeing again? Who are we to judge the sorrow of others? The desires to be reunited with them?'

Joshua immediately stopped his work. His arms dropped as memories of the past hauntingly remerged. 'You know what I love about Savannah the most? She has my mother's heart. Actually, she's just like her. The same radiant complexion, the same strength of character. It's probably why my dad liked Sav so much.' Fond memories forged a smile on his face. 'Dad would often travel abroad on missionary work, leaving me behind with her. He spent a lot of time in Africa, and one time, I was left with relatives while my mom went to visit him. And that was when my world changed. My mother called me crying, there was all kinds of screaming in the background. It was hard to make out what was going on. She just kept saying "I'll always be with you; I'll always be with you". I was just a child, but I knew—' Joshua paused, unable to say the words. 'I kept telling her that I want to be with her… asking where she was. I would have done anything to be able to just get to her at that time when she needed me. And yes, I would do anything to be with her now. That was the day I lost my faith. A world with such cruelty could never be of divine design.'

The old man saw the flood building up behind Joshua's eyelids. 'I think I understand now. Joshua, I've been hesitant to say this, because of where we are and because of what I've done but… I've realized that accepting both the emotions of what we gain and lose in life defines what we are and *who* we are—'

'Please, don't say what you're going to say,' Joshua frowned heavily as he shot out a glare of fury at Hannerman; something was ignited inside of him. His arms tensed. 'You think I can just turn my emotions off?'

'No, but that you must deal with it, and have a purpose beyond your despair.'

'Every minute of the day, all I can feel is pain,' Joshua's voice broke from the truth he could no longer keep at bay. 'No matter what I do, no matter what I eat or drink, the feeling doesn't go away. I'm so depressed, I want to sleep all day, but I can't because of the thought of waking up to Savannah not being there. I keep thinking, what if I didn't make her run away that night? What if I had only listened to her?'

'What happened to your mother and Savannah was not your fault Joshua. Don't let guilt ruin your life.'

Despite the old man's sound advice, it couldn't close the flood gates of Joshua's anguish which he'd been trying to contain. 'Without her, I don't want a life. I don't want to be haunted by a shadow, by memories. You're going to tell me to be thankful for the time we shared together? Huh?' he shouted. 'I can't be, because I want more.'

'Look, I'm not saying to give up on Savannah. But your focus is off, you look awful, you're not taking care of yourself. Things might not happen as quickly as you want and you'll kill yourself before ever finding her if you don't learn to accept that losing people we love is a part of life.'

Joshua sobbed, holding his face in his right palm. 'I miss her, Frank. I miss her so much. I lost my best friend.' He wiped his tears before speaking again.

'I know, I know how it feels.'

'Will it ever go away? The pain?'

Hannerman struggled as he thought of his reply. 'Not really. Time does help to bury the memories and emotions deeper inside and you might not think of the loss for days, months… but it always comes back. Your time with Savannah was the best years of your life. But my wife and I were friends since I was nine years old, we got married at eighteen… she *was* my life. How could I ever stop missing her?'

'So how do you deal with it?'

'I deal with it knowing that she would have wanted me to be happy, and that my tragedy should not determine who I am, at least not detrimentally. That I should use it to help others and try to make this big scary world a not-so-big and not-so-scary place for future generations. I tell myself, *Frank, you're going to be ok*. I guess I'm kind of hoping she's looking down at me and smiling every time I do something good.'

Joshua sniffled. 'Looking down from where?'

Hannerman raised a pointed finger. 'Don't say it.'

'I was going to say like a tall ladder or a tree.'

They laughed together. Something then caught the older man's attention as he looked at the levitated display.

'I believe the machine is ready,' Hannerman said.

***

More than an hour had passed, and the Quantum Room was packed with scientists and security personnel. Dr. Hannerman, Moreau and Joshua took center stage, along with a layered vision view of the Control Room, where Marcs and his personnel were energized with prep activity. The view of the Control Room was like peering through a wide, rectangular window. To the side of it was another floating image, this one of satellite images of the Ring and both towers.

For their first attempt at interplanetary biological teleportation, they aimed to send two worms to Olympus. But the Lithium-Obsidian power cells had been depleted by their experiments. They had to acquire more energy.

'We're ready to fire up the space generator as soon as you give the word,' Hannerman said to Moreau.

Moreau gave him a nod. 'Colonel Marcs, proceed!' Moreau ordered in his stiff stance, arms behind his back.

'Acknowledged.' Colonel Marcs replied on the room's comms. He uttered the ancient Greek phrase and the Control Room's staff repeated it back, and the chorus of their voices via the Quantum Room's speakers engulfed Joshua. 'Major, demagnetize the camps.'

'I can confirm the Ring and towers are now detached,' the major said. The colonel's second in command sat in his seat in front of the viewing screen and aform input consoles while Marcs hung over him.

Joshua kept both eyes focused on the view of the Ring dreading what was yet to come.

He glanced at Zahurska biting her lips as she viewed the layered vision imagery of the Ring wrapped around the Earth like an intrinsic metallic belt around its waist. 'I've seen the sims, but this is the first time I'm witnessing the energy harvest. It's giving me goosebumps.'

'It should,' Joshua said.

'I'm not quite sure how it all works.' She kept her comments low enough for only Joshua to hear—an easy feat among the background noise.

'Begin the next phase,' Moreau ordered. 'Activate thrusters.'

'Brace yourselves,' said Hannerman.

The noise level suddenly magnified. Joshua's body, along with every person there was jolted by the force of a change in velocity. He caught Zahurska as she stumbled like a train passenger to a change in momentum.

'It's alright,' he said to her after she released a subtle yelp.

'We're speeding up?' Zahurska said.

Joshua's stomach was a meatgrinder, churning at the thought of what they were doing. He felt that perhaps explaining things to her would help both of their ordeals. 'No, we're slowing down. Now that the Ring has been detached from the towers, it's orbiting Earth at a matching speed. It needs to decelerate for power generation. We've turned the Earth into one giant homopolar generator. It converts the planet's kinetic energy into electrical energy. The towers are stators and the Ring is really two parallel rails loaded with silver conducting coils along its entire length. At the tops of the towers are massive magnets, and as they spin, the magnets induce an electric current in the coils via linear induction.'

'And we store this charge in the world's largest battery bank,' Moreau said, eavesdropping. He came up close to Joshua's ear. 'This should be a proud moment for you; to see your ambitions realized.'

Joshua didn't have the words for a response.

It wasn't long before it felt like the entire facility shook as the Ring fired up its ion rockets and began a prograde spin around the Earth. The power storage system generated a spine-chilling hiss as the energy flowing through them made a rumble. Earth spun on its axis, and that spin is what kept water at the equator. Their action would cause more of the world's oceans to move towards the poles.

For what shall it profit a man, if he shall gain the whole world, and lose his own soul? Joshua remembered the bible verse from his father's teaching, now he began to realize painfully what it meant. By activating the space generator, they were slowing down the Earth's rotation; Mother Nature would be delivering her wrath across the globe. There would have been instant volcanic eruptions, more earthquakes; tsunamis would be inundating coastlines. Many would die. He hated what he had become. *How much was one woman worth,* he thought. *Was she worth the lives of millions?*

'Energy storage capacity is at optimal levels,' said one of the colonel's personnel.

'Deactivate the energy harvest,' Moreau said. A few minute's worth was enough energy needed for their trial. 'Initiate the prograde spin, Colonel.'

'Affirmative!' Colonel Marcs patted the shoulder of his executive officer. 'You heard the man. Let's bring the goose back home to roost. Power on the ion thrusters.'

Joshua heard the countdown, and as soon as it was over, came the tug of acceleration. He held his belly, both his travel sickness and his guilt giving him nausea. He hoped no one had noticed.

'Dr. Smith,' Moreau said. 'If you're feeling up to it, perhaps now that we have the power you wouldn't mind preceding with the Quantum Transender trial.'

With mixed emotions, Joshua glanced at Jonahs, Van DeMay and Zahursha who were all awaiting his instructions. He gave Zahurska the nod to place the Petri dish containing the earthworm specimens onto the main quantum transcender's platform. They all watched as she placed the worms at the center of the circular superconductive plate integrated into the glass floor.

After she had made it to a safe distance, he activated the machine. The ultrafaron metal ring floated upwards from five to seven and a half feet in the air. They ran through each phase of the sequence.

'Magnetic field's reached a hundred teslas and rapidly climbing,' Jonahs said. The Petri dish's immediate levitation was a testament to his findings. 'One thousand teslas,' he turned to Joshua, his face pale, mouth hung open. 'Four thousand teslas.'

Hannerman leaned toward Moreau. 'That's the strongest man-made magnetic field ever created, stronger than we've generated before.'

The information had somewhat of a negative effect on the room's personnel. Some backed away fearing the worse was to come. But Joshua maintained his conviction. 'Initiate the energy pulse,' he ordered Dr. Jonahs, 'on three, two, one, pulse.'

From above, a non-evanescent beam of intense white energy struck the floating ultrafaron. After seconds passed, the beam vanished, and the conductive ring generated a massive orb of blue, translucent light as the Teleporter sucked the power from the energy storage cells. Objects close to the orb began to elevate as it disrupted gravity around it. Aware of the effects, the personnel in the room all wore magnetic boots to anchor them to the reinforced glass floor courtesy of magnetic coils which laid underneath. It was just precautionary, as the magnetic field should have been contained within the machine. Staring through the orb, the room witnessed the worms disappearing. The orb abruptly dispersed, and the gravitational pull of the machine stopped.

'Did it work?' Mr. Moreau asked.

'Standard deviation measures…,' Zahurska paused, her jaw hung as she turned to Joshua.

'What is it?' Moreau asked again, with more agitation.

'Sorry sir, according to my readings, SD measures… seven

sigma.'

'Incredible!' uttered Hannerman, the measurement had the same contagious effect on the mouths of all the scientists in the room.

'I'm not interested in your measurements,' Moreau said. 'Did the Olympus teleportation work or not?'

With Joshua stunned by what had transpired, Hannerman felt it best to explain to the group the significance of the revelation.

'Ladies and gentlemen, the Sigma level is a measure of how confident scientists feel their results are. Seven sigma is the highest level probability of accuracy in physics. No scientific experiment in the history of civilization has had this level of certainty, including my soul teleportation model, nor my mind correction code.'

Smiles and claps lit up the room, mostly aimed at Joshua who struggled to take it all in. An alarm sounded, quelling the young genius' adulation. The lights turned red, bringing the applauds to an abrupt stop.

'Someone tell me what's happening,' Joshua said. No one looked at him as they all tried to make sense of the facility's warning systems.

'You've done something wrong, *again*,' Moreau shouted over the alarm.

'No,' Joshua shook his head confused by it all. 'We didn't make any mistakes. The worms were Teleported.'

'Red alert, this is Dogpatch actual, I need all Ghost Teams at ready status,' Colonel Marcs said on the facility-wide communications speaker. 'This is not a drill. I repeat, red alert, this is Dogpatch actual, all Ghost Teams at ready status. Quantum Room, Mr. Moreau, Dr. Hannerman are you receiving, over.'

'Yes, Colonel Marcs,' Hannerman said, 'why are we at red alert?'

'We have a breach—within the facility.'

CHAPTER FOUR

THE OATH
'Watch over her father, be her shepherd and guide her soul to where you deem it worthy. We are in the time of Armageddon, and your loyal servants stand at the ready to do your will.'

The man of God sat by Savannah's bedside among rows of thousands of Unknown, speaking words few would dare utter in public. The building had finally stopped moving after a massive quake, but the Hive's lighting hadn't returned to its normal brightness. Some of the medical monitoring equipment refused to turn back on and pandemonium infected the staff as they frantically dashed around.

He held her cold hands and rubbed them to provide warmth, remembering the countless times she came to see him. Joshua never accompanied her, but there was the odd occasion the reverend would glance out of the window, and Joshua would be waiting outside on an Octopede's back. She had his wife's grace; she had to have her stubbornness as well. Savannah continuously spoke of her attempts to get Joshua to make amends with his father. But despite his son's disdain, she never stopped checking up on the old man's health and making sure he was well fed.

The bang of the door being opened would have stolen the concentration of most men but did little to startle Joshua's father from his prayers. Dr. Panesar was panting like he had run up flights of stairs.

'What are you doing?' he said to the old black male. 'I saw that.

That's illegal.'

The reverend was determined to finish what he started. 'She is precious to us my Lord, if a life must be sacrificed for your mercy, I would gladly take her place. Protect her soul, amen.'

'I can get into trouble if I don't inform the authorities.'

'Do what you must, while he is with me, I fear nothing. But it looks like you have more important matters to attend to.'

Dr. Panesar took a brief moment to catch his breath and push his slipping glasses back up his nose. 'You need to leave.'

'I think not.'

'The quake has knocked out our power and damaged most of our backup generators.'

'What are your plans, doctor? Are you abandoning your patients?'

He puffed. 'No. At least... not all of them. We don't have enough emergency power to keep life support running. And without the generators... the UPS' will hold out for another hour at best, then the Hive ward will go dark.'

'Ah,' the reverend said softly, almost to a whisper. 'Just the Unknowns. No point wasting precious power on those with little chance of life.'

'Look, this is terrible, I know. I've been caring for some of these patients for years. I don't want to do this either. But it's out of my hands, the decision's been made. Tell her husband, Dr. Smith, I'm sorry. There's nothing else I can do. This is the hardest decision I've ever had to make in my career.'

'It's good that it is, but it is not necessary.'

'Not necessary?'

'Doctor Panesar,' a nurse said from afar. She had been running around hectically in the background, trying to organize the other medical staff.

'Yes Vicky.'

'We're ready to relocate the equipment when you say the word,' said the nurse.

'The equipment is staying where it is, Vicky,' the reverend said with authority.

'Excuse me?' the nurse said.

'So are you,' said Rev. Smith.

'Look, sir, we didn't make the call,' Panesar said.

'Perhaps that's true, but it's relevant. These people need your help.'

'So do hundreds of others who we can actually treat and heal. Power or no power, Miss Jenkins probably has less than seventy-two hours—'

'God alone shall decide her time on this Earth, not your medical estimates.'

'Mr. Smith.' The doctor's voice elevated to a newfound height. The pressure of the situation made him breathe as heavy as when he first entered. 'There is little we can do now for these patients.'

Rev. Smith got up slowly. He kissed Savannah on the cheek softly before taking his sweet time to approach Dr. Panesar and the nurse.

'We both swore an oath to what we believe in, doctor. Yours was the Hippocratic oath. *"Into whatsoever houses I enter, I will enter to help the sick, and I will abstain from all intentional wrong-doing and harm, especially from abusing the bodies of man or woman, bond or free."* You swore to do no harm, doctor. Despite my persecution from the intolerant and personal tragedies, I have not abandoned my oath. Do not be so quick to abandon yours.'

A flash of darkness covered them, closely followed by sounds of electronic machines depowering and the panic of medical staff.

'Where is your God now?' Dr. Panesar said in the dark.

CHAPTER FIVE

HUNTED
Chaos took hold.

Half of the Quantum Room rushed for the exit, some stood still, while others moved backwards, placing their backs to the walls. The neo-humans were invisible, and the eyes of the personnel all frightfully searched every corner of the Quantum Room, bracing for an assault. After the initial screams, the room quieted, each person hoping to not draw attention to themselves.

Joshua backed away from the Transcender, he figured it was the most likely location of the creature. But there was only so far his legs would allow him to move. He was paralyzed more by the memory of Savannah's attack than by his current threat. Yells for him to flee from standing alone in the center rung in his ear; it originated from Jonahs of all people.

'Where is the breach, Colonel?' Moreau said in a panting panic. He stood behind his R-MEN guards along with Hannerman.

'We're attempting to identify now, but it is not in the Quantum Room.'

Unbearable tension exhaled in their shared relief. Moreau reacted quickly, roaring at the security staff to lock the entrance and stand guard. 'Was it your goal to bring them here, Smith?' Moreau yelled.

Hannerman interrupted him in Joshua's defense. 'We have always experienced a strengthened Quantum entanglement with Olympus surrounding the Ring whenever we teleported souls, and we predicted this could happen one day.'

'Yet it's never happened,' Moreau snapped.

'Indeed,' agreed the neuroscientist, 'but we have never teleported matter before. The breach is consistent with the evidence that the worms made it to Olympus and the experiment was a success. Colonel Marcs, what's the current situation?'

'We have identified there are at least two hostiles inside the facility.'

'Goodness me!' Joshua said, forced to listen in fright as he remembered the power of the creatures, and he had only encountered one.

'All Ghost Teams get to the armory immediately,' Colonel Marcs ordered. 'One hostile located in the canteen area, section 12. We've got people being ripped to shreds down there. Haul ass!'

The colonel's words stunned the Quantum Room.

'Where is the other one, colonel?' Moreau asked.

'We have no confirmed location on the other hostile. This facility has the circumference of the equator, that's forty thousand kilometers to seek and destroy.'

Hannerman replied, 'It will be close, colonel. Send teams to secure the Quantum Room, we cannot allow them through here. If we lose the Quantum Transcender, we lose all hope.'

'Acknowledged! Standby, we're relaying our security footage to your layered vision display.'

The augmented reality Screen, as well as the physical monitors, displayed the carnage. The screams and weapons fire rendered it difficult to understand any words. One of the scientists in the room fainted. The utter horror of an invisible creature slaughtering all the personnel in the canteen was too much for many to bare. After it had finished hunting down those that tried to flee, the neo-human ransacked the mess deck with its brutish strength.

'I'm reading fires and hull fractures in multiple locations within section 12,' Zahurska reported. 'We're going to start losing atmosphere.'

Van DeMay looked petrified, Jonahs' emotional dial never changed from its default setting, but Joshua sensed a difference in Zahurska. While she appeared shaken up by past incidents, she had emerged from it a changed woman. Her voice was commanding, speaking to the science personnel like a general marshaling her troops.

'Could we lockdown sections eleven to thirteen and jettison compartment 12?' Dr. Hannerman said.

'We're not scuttling this facility,' Moreau snapped. 'If Smith has succeeded, then we must send teams to Olympus immediately and complete the mission before it's too late.'

'Are you insane?' Joshua said, Moreau's guards flicked their robotic heads as if they didn't take kindly to Joshua's outcry. 'There are people dying down there.'

'In order to harness the Earth's rotational energy,' Moreau said, 'we need the Ring intact.'

***

Ghost Team One made it to the armory along with operators belonging to other Ghost Teams. Black Knight led the pack; he flung the battery pack of his tech-rifle on his back and connected its four black cables to the weapon with less haste than the others. Wingman and Peacemaker franticly snatched and grabbed their gear, while the silent giant, The Boogieman, used his hulking arms to lift up the massive weapon that sent the creature that attacked Joshua back to the depths from whence it came.

'Patrón,' Loca called out to Tombstone. He waved at her to come closer. Even in a firefight, she paid more attention to sensor display and the team's radio communication and she had been listening in on the other Ghost Team chatter. Some had already engaged the neo-humans.

'Talk to me!' the Polish man uttered in quick reply.

'Team Four has been wiped out from the sounds of it.'

'Just keep monitoring the comms,' he replied, before throwing her weapon at her chest which she caught awkwardly. 'It doesn't change a thing. We've got a job to do. Dogpatch, this is Ghost Team One Actual. Do you copy? Over.' Tombstone spoke into his wireless transceiver. In the distance, they heard the faint screams of personnel. It made Peacemaker swear at another combat soldier to get out of his way.

'Copy Ghost Team One,' Marcs replied. 'We have you at the armory, give me a sitrep. Over.'

'Sir, we are armed, we have a soul redeemer and are on our way to engage hostile in section 12. Over.'

'Acknowledged. Revert that son of a bitch off my facility

immediately. That is not a polite suggestion, soldier.'

Wingman threw Tombstone an ammunition belt, he grabbed it without looking, focusing on Loca's tablet as its sensors searched for the creatures.

'Wilco, Colonel. Tombstone, out.' The broad Sergeant addressed his team as he prepped his advance weapon. 'Listen up. Only short bursts of controlled weapons-fire. Our ammunition can easily rupture the hull, and for you geniuses that haven't noticed, we don't have spacesuits. Peacemaker, if I see any wild firing, I'm going to throw you out of a fucking airlock.'

'Yo Sarge,' Wingman said. 'We only got one drone; the other GTs took the rest of them.'

'Piece of fucking shits!' Tombstone said, accompanied by a stream of expletives in his native tongue.

Wingman activated a black cube and flung the UAV into the air. As soon as it released from his grasp, its flight mode activated. Four propellers appeared as it transformed into an aerodynamic shape.

In a blink, darkness descended on them. They moaned and swore, unable to see so much as their hands in front of them. The Boogieman's weapon and Loca's tablet were their only source of lighting until they got their helmets and shoulder torches operational.

'Dogpatch, this is GT1,' Tombstone said. 'Please be advised, we have a power outage. Over.'

'Acknowledged, GT1,' Marcs said, 'you must proceed with the reversion. Lions do their best hunting at night. Over.'

'Affirmative, Colonel,' Tombstone replied.

'This is some shit,' Wingman said after a deep huff.

'Sergeant, request permission to leave,' Black Knight said in his usual calmness.

'What the fuck, Black?' Wingman said. 'Where you gotta go? You looking after your sick fucking grandmother?'

'Nah he's chicken shit scared that's all,' Peacemaker said with a devilish grin.

Despite this comment, he knew they were not surprised by his request. He had instinct for bloodshed and could sense it coming like a summer rain. 'I need to stop the other creature before it is too late.'

'Fuck you mean too late?' Tombstone said. His English

degenerated whenever his blood pressure increased.

'It's headed to the machine.'

'How would your sorry ass know that, homeboy?' Peacemaker said, his pale face had gone red in anxiousness and aggression.

As crazy as Tombstone thought he was, the Sergeant knew Black Knight was never wrong when he called it. Two facility personnel ran past them bloodied and bruised; one dragging their left leg.

Wingman grabbed the injured woman, shinning his torchlight into her petrified eyes. 'Calm down lady, where the hell is it?'

Hysterical, the woman attacked him ferociously to force him to let go of her. Peacemaker pulled his cutlass out and imprinted it on her face, her slight movement made it cut her cheek.

'Easy honey,' Peacemaker said with a gentle voice. The woman immediately calmed to the more direct threat. 'Better start talking.'

As she sobbed, the aerial drone drifted ahead of them as programmed.

'Guys, look!' Loca, her sight narrowed onto the drone as its LEDs blinked rapidly in a monotonous warning tone.

Peacemaker saw it too, and slowly released the lady to put his hand back on his weapon. 'You've bought a friend.'

'The drone's picking up movement,' Tombstone said.

They pointed their weapons, slowly spreading themselves across the width of the corridor. While the team tried to use their layered vision and flashlights to identify anything they could, Black Knight bent down low and let his fingertips touch the floor; listening to what it told him.

'Get ready,' Black Knight uttered. 'It's coming.'

Wingman stepped back; his weapon rattled against his body from the suspense.

The sound of multiple poundings on the hull made the team stagger backwards in fright. The floor indented, and the damage drew rapidly nearer.

'Contact!' Tombstone yelled for the world to hear.

As the creature rushed at them, releasing an echoing roar, they opened fire. The resonating rounds shot from their weapons' parallel plates of their barrels made the creature flee in agony. Black Knight had to shake off the effects of the ringing in his ear due to the firefight's acoustics reverberating against the Ring's hull.

'Dogpatch, we are in pursuit of hostile one. Black Knight and

Loca are tracking down the second hostile.' Tombstone snapped his head back to the dark soldier. 'You two, get going, now!' The Sergeant and the rest his team took off in chase. Wingman stepped over the mutilated bodies of dead Ghost Team operators, yet Peacemaker seemed nonchalant about his boot coming down on a corpse's face.

Moving swiftly through the Ring's empty corridors, Tombstone swung around a corner and witnessed two Ghost Team operators engaged in battle with the creature. They held a replica of The Boogieman's weapon, but without his powerful build, they stood on each side of it to deal with its heavy weight.

Ghost Team One watched the ferocious onslaught of the creature as its silhouette ripped through the men before their weapon had a chance to do significant damage. When it was finished with one of the men, an invisible force flung the soldier against the Ring's bulkhead wall with such strength, the reinforced metal indented, and the soldier died upon impact. Another blow from the neo-human knocked the second soldier's head off his body. The monster then crashed through an airlock door into another section of the facility, and the team tried hopelessly to keep up with its speed.

Observers watched on from the Quantum Room in fear of the chaos. Hannerman called a senior guard over. 'Get a repair crew to stabilize section 15 before we lose the whole compartment.'

'The creature is heading towards the main power substation,' Moreau said with a shaky voice. 'Any explosion in there could ignite the coils' liquid helium coolant and cascade, the installation will be inoperable.'

'Colonel Marcs,' Hannerman said. 'Your men must eliminate the threat quickly; it will be at power substation H soon. If it damages the power station and that does not instantly kill us, it will still completely black out half of the Ring's circumference.'

'Acknowledged, doctor,' Marcs said, managing operations in the control room. His subordinates darted franticly around him, all of them armed to the teeth. But their conventional rifles and sidearms had little effect on their foes. Knowing this, Marcs remained composed—as though he ate bad news for breakfast. He hunched over his executive officer's desk. 'But I've got a skeleton detachment up here, Hannerman. Most of our forces are on deployment on Earth, this breach has taken us completely off guard and we still can't locate the second hostile.' The colonel surveyed the multiple CCTV feeds to locate his men.

'Colonel,' called his executive officer seated at his station. 'I can't reach any other Ghost Teams on the station. They're either MIA or KIA. Only Ghost Team One is left.'

Marcs kept his eyes fixed on the screens. 'I hope you've packed your wetsuit, Major. Because we're swimming in the shit now.'

***

Joshua found himself mirroring the rest of the room; locked in silence, they stared at the security camera footage. He saw Tombstone, Peacemaker and Wingman pinning the creature down with their hail of bullets, and The Boogieman finally caught up with them, toting the heavy weapon. While the others held their breath in suspense, Joshua kept trying to think of how he could help. A sudden realization made him jump and grab Hannerman's shoulder. 'We need to capture one of them alive.'

'Don't be ridiculous,' Moreau said.

'You need to test that the mind-code actually works on a live specimen, we don't know how many second chances we'll get.' With the intensity of the moment, Joshua didn't mind raising his tone to the ghostly pale man whose face still constantly dripped a liquid substance.

Hannerman nodded his head in agreement. 'Cagliostro, he's right. We cannot afford to fail.' Hannerman grabbed a security personnel's radio. 'Colonel Marcs, for our mission to work we need one of the creatures alive.'

'Are you shitting me?' Marcs barked on the radio.

***

Along the corridors, the neo-human roared in a hellish vocal tone that would chill a nerve worse than chalk on an old school blackboard. Their barrage caused it tremendous pain, but it still refused to die with the utmost contempt. Each round they fired lit up a tiny spot of the neo-human's body upon impact, creating a spectral image of the giant creature.

'Now Boogieman!' Tombstone said.

The dark goliath released his weapon's charge and its purple beam slammed into the creature. It yelled in utter agony. A translucent orb emerged disrupting gravity and lifting Tombstone, Wingman and Peacemaker in the air. The tremendous heat made the air sizzle and partially seared Tombstone's face as his body floated toward the blinding light. He squinted to his side, relieved to see The Boogieman still on his feet; his near four hundred pounds in addition to his weapon's bulky mass anchored him down.

'Don't let up,' Peacemaker screamed. His palms slid along the ceiling of the corridor, his fingernails gripping the tiny grooves of the panels as he yelled and fired.

Seconds later came a reverberating bang. The energy ball vanished, and they crashed to the ground.

'Rupture in the hull,' Wingman shouted, shaking off the pain of banging his head on the metal ground. 'Get the fuck out of here.'

Tombstone watched the Asian soldier dashing towards the section's airlock. His weapon was sucked out into space as the oxygen rapidly escaped. He had about ten to fifteen seconds before his deoxygenated blood circulated from his lungs to his brain and he blacked out. Following the rest of his men, the Sergeant sprinted to safety.

'Control Room,' Tombstone said into his transceiver. 'We've lost atmosphere in section 16.' Needing to breathe, the scarred operator couldn't say anything else.

Peacemaker shoved Wingman in his shoulder. 'I thought I heard you crying like a lil' bitch, homeboy. Smells like you've pissed your pants.'

'Go fuck yourself, Corporal,' the athletic-built soldier replied. 'It was a close shave, something you could do with, you ugly bastard.' Both men had lost their weapon fleeing from the rupture.

Now in the calm, they heard the colonel's voice on the comms link.

'Ghost Team One, please respond, I repeat, we need the creatures alive do you understand me? Over.'

Peacemaker immediately switched off his mic. 'Whiskey Tango Foxtrot? Has the colonel lost his monkey-ass mind?'

'Colonel Marcs, sir,' the Sergeant replied, he paused to catch his breath. 'That order was not received in time; we've reverted the soul. Over.'

The colonel sighed deeply on their radio channel before

breaking out into a swearing fit.

'But sir,' Tombstone said. 'Black Knight and Loca are tracking the other creature.'

***

Black Knight and Loca cautiously maneuvered through the dark corridors focusing on minimizing their noise level rather than maximizing their speed; stepping sometimes awkwardly on the bullet shell casing and personal items shattered on the floor. Loca's tablet trembled in her left hand, yet her face was a flood of rage, both fear and conviction exhaled with every breath she released. Black Knight looked calm and determined in each step. They crept forward at an angle so to avoid an ambush from a rear attack. Dismembered bodies indicated they were following a deadly trail.

A sudden rasp on their radio transceivers alerted them.

'Black Knight, Loca, come in, this Dogpatch actual,' Marcs said.

'We're reading you, sir,' Loca replied quietly. 'Five by Five.'

'Where is the other target? Over.'

'It is headed for the Quantum Room, sir. Over,' Black Knight whispered as sweat rolled down to his unkempt beard.

'Black Knight, this is Dr. Frank Hannerman. We need this creature alive and you're our only hope. To capture it, force it into the containment cells on section twenty-two. We are counting on you.'

'Acknowledged!' he said without flinching. 'Open all the containment cell doors, now, over.'

When Loca heard Hannerman's words, she stopped in her tracks. 'With no drones, we don't have a sensor grid, Caballero.'

'I know,' Black Knight said, unfazed.

'So my GCD's motion sensors are picking up movement all over the place, but I can't pinpoint the signatures with any accuracy without the UAVs.'

'I know.' His yellow eyes full of brown pigment remained focused ahead.

Loca looked at him, puffing hard to compose herself. His iron-like concentration was a warning signal; from past missions, it predicted danger earlier than her tech. 'Negro,' she called out, knowing to keep her voice low. 'It's going to see us before we see it, and we don't have The Boogieman here or a redeemer.'

'No need,' the tall man said. 'I can hunt it. Stay close. It is not far.'

Back in the Quantum Room, Joshua felt a sense of hopelessness as they waited in suspense. In the wave of panic that consumed the minds of the room, his thoughts lingered on the next step ahead. If he were to be successful in finding Savannah's soul, he needed to be sure the mind code worked. His concern was the Ghost Teams. If it meant their deaths, they wouldn't hesitate to destroy the creature to defend themselves. 'I just hope they don't kill it,' he uttered aloud.

'The creatures cannot be killed, Dr. Smith,' Moreau said. 'The most we can do is temporarily immobilize them or perform a reversion. They were created to live forever.'

'So, what do the Ghost Team's weapons fire?' Joshua asked.

Hannerman intervened. 'Their primary weapon, we call it the MKEPX13, a miniaturized kinetic energy penetrator rifle. It uses ultrafaron-titanium alloy bullets forged from ultrafarite ore, and fragments of the creature's own exoskeletons which we collect from any shards of their bodies broken off after a reversion. Before that, the first time we brought one down was with a tank's 120-millimeter gun.'

'And what about the other weapon? The one that looks big and heavy?'

'We call it the soul redeemer,' Hannerman said. 'It's a magnetic Higgs—'

'Magnetic Higgs boson frequency disruptor,' Joshua interrupted.

'Correct. It's the only weapon that can pull the souls of the neo-humans back to Olympus where we believe they are not destroyed but then given a new body.' Hannerman watched how the young physicist stroked his chin in deep thought. 'If you have a plan let's hear it?'

'The soul redeemer has just given me an idea.' He jumped on to a computer terminal, pushing Dr. Jonahs to the side in his haste. 'Zahurska, Van DeMay, I need your assistance. You too, Frank.'

'What's your plan, sir?' Van DeMay asked in a thick lisp.

'You saturated Earth's atmosphere with Higgs bosons. We need to do the same to the facility's atmosphere.'

''What good with that do?' Dr. Jonahs said, no doubt annoyed that he was excluded from Joshua's request for help.

'I'm going to alter the frequency at which the Higgs particles change into other subatomic particles.'

Hannerman accessed the Higgs boson containment tanks systems via AR projection commands with finger gestures and prepped to release the particles.

'What exactly are you doing, Smith?' Moreau asked. 'We have little time for your games right now.'

Joshua snapped back, angry but contained. 'Look, I'm altering our stored Higgs particles to a different frequency harmonic to the ones in the neo-human's body, ok?'

'No! For what forsaken purpose?'

'Destructive Interference,' Dr. Jonahs said with a hint of displeasure.

'That's the theory,' Joshua said. 'It should interfere with the bosons in the neo-human's body and hopefully, cause it to become visible. That way we can find it and hopefully secure it.'

***

Black Knight and Loca followed the screams and littered dead, slowing their speed down more to a creep. A rasp on the radio transceiver that hung by their ears disrupted their stealthy movement.

'Mr. Black Knight, do you read me? Over,' a voice on his comms link said, louder against the surrounding silence than the soldier would have liked.

'Smith!' Black Knight replied, in his predominantly British accent. His face distorted upon recognition.

'We've flooded the corridors with particles that will allow the creature to be seen.'

The rugged man maintained his forward creep. 'I don't need to see it to hunt it.'

'Please, we need it alive.'

'Listen to me,' Black Knight whispered. 'The containment cell will not be strong enough to hold the creature. When I give the word, I need you to turn off the gravity in deck twenty-two. Do you hear me?'

'Yes, yes I understand. We're working on it now.'

Black Knight turned to Loca. 'How are we doing with the cell doors, Loca?'

'Colonel Marcs says all the doors are open. We...' A sound broke her sentence. He looked behind but saw nothing in the darkness. 'Black... my sister, she's a neo-human. That's why I'm here. If anything happens to me, I want you to find her for me. Find and give her this.' She lifted a chain out from her black combat uniform and revealed a pendant. It was digitized; the blue of its LCDs glistened in the darkness. 'Promise me.'

He nodded. Her lips parted, but the bearded man placed a coarse finger over her mouth before she could speak again and remained dead still. Loca stopped in her tracks also. He looked directly down at the metal walkway with an unbreakable focus.

'What is it? Talk to me?' she asked.

'Now we... are the ones being hunted. Don't make any sudden moves.'

Loca flinched. Sweat dripped off her jawline like someone had splashed her with water. Her eyes were reflective from the swelling liquid, but no tears fell. 'Say the word, Caballero,' her speech began weak, but strengthened when she remembered all that she had survived. 'Let's do this.' She kept nodding, confirming her conviction to him. There was no way she would let his bravery outshine her own.

'We have the prey, and we have the trap; all we need now is bait.'

Her heart sank in that moment—she trusted him, but feared she was the bait he referred to.

Black Knight locked his eyes onto hers, the imminent threat couldn't break his gaze. 'When I say run, get to the cells. Don't look back, just run faster than you've ever had to in your life.' He held her shoulders and felt her trembling. But fear was never something he had known her to vocalize, such was her pride. Instead, her eyes were a raging tempest of aggression, and she nodded in smaller, faster movements.

Slowly, he lowered his hand and held his weapon. 'Run!' he yelled.

Loca took off, hoping she wouldn't be racing to sudden death. In seconds, the bulkhead wall behind Black Knight broke apart. Gas expelled from a damaged pipe, pushing a gray mist in the air.

The man stood still, it was the first time in all his years as a Ghost Team operator that he had seen the true form of a neo-human with his own eyes, outside of a computer-simulated construct. This was no spectral form, no translucent image—thanks to Joshua's intervention, he saw a sight he had wished to never—ever witness.

Its skin was like a super hard, extra-muscled exoskeleton, and stood over eight feet tall even with its natural hunched posture. Its head was hideous, embedded with five tiny, beady red eyes, all of them trained on him. The eyes glowed, piercing through the darkness and searching for his soul to claim it. Curved, horn-like structures on its skull seemed to shift their position at will. There was no distinguishable nose, but a mouth that opened vertically up to half of its face and closed similarly to the ebb and flow of waves on shore; exposing black, jagged shards of what must have been teeth. It took one step toward him and its foot's downward weight boomed through the corridor.

Bred his whole life for war, Black Knight felt he'd seen every horror this Earth held. But this horror was not of Earth, and for the first time in his life since he was a boy, he experienced the curse of fear. 'On the day I called, you answered me,' he uttered quietly to himself, his voice unyielding and unshaken. 'You made me bold with strength... in my soul.' The creature took another big step towards him like a stalking predator, poised, ready to pounce. It released a hissing sound that made his body turn cold. His limbs began to seize up, it was like the sound drained the life from him; the spirit from him. It opened and closed its oversized hand repeatedly, the arm attached to it, grotesque in its massive form.

'Come,' Black Knight said. Still and resolute in his posture.

Suddenly he squeezed the trigger and bolted. The creature gave chase, crushing the metal corridor floor and it roared from the bullet wounds. The high-impact rounds made cracks in its exoskeleton—yet it kept gaining. Running as fast as he could, he couldn't get a proper aim. It closed the distance on the man with a speed that would catch him at any moment.

Loca made it to the containment cell and closed the door, and soon after Black Knight reached the second containment cell opposite, sliding across the floor when he attempted to stop himself. He leaped inside as it caught up to him. The neo-human stalked inside, slowing, knowing its prey was cornered. It peered inside the eight by five meters squared holding room then stepped in after him. It released a sound like a cobra's hiss synthesized, its giant mass consuming the room.

'Now Smith!' Black Knight said.

He quickly released his weapon and used his fingernails to grip onto the tiny grooves and indentations in the metal floor. The cell lost its gravity along with the entire eight hundred meters cylindrical, modular section of the facility. The creature began to float and roared so loudly it was sure to cause lasting trauma to his eardrums. Using his arms, the soldier propelled himself underneath the struggling creature as it spun involuntarily, and he exited the cell.

'Loca, close the cell, now,' he yelled.

His command was unnecessary, she saw him floating out from the narrow viewing glass and instantly closed the cell.

'Ingenious!' Joshua said, looking on from the Quantum Room via the security camera footage on the monitors. 'Without gravity the creature can't effectively apply its strength.'

'I'll prep the mind code,' Hannerman said.

'Whatever you gentlemen are up to you'd better do it fast,' Marcs said via the intercom. 'All available units report to the containment cells in section twenty-two.'

'Colonel Marcs,' Moreau said.

'Yes sir.'

'There must be a nationwide recall of all Ghost Teams effective immediately.'

CHAPTER SIX

MONSTROUS REFLECTION

Joshua and Hannerman made their way to the holding area within the Ring's section twenty-two. Their slower and abnormal movement was thanks to the magnetic boots they wore, which kept them from floating. Yet the electronics did not result in the smoothest of motion. Joshua had to practice walking in them for a while first, being mindful to not have both feet off the floor at the same time.

They were met by rows of Ghost Team operators who filed in on each side of the corridor. Pounding noises intensified as Joshua and Hannerman stopped at the contingent of soldiers surrounding Colonel Marcs who were fully armed and on edge.

'Your friend doesn't sound too happy in there, Dr. Smith,' the colonel said. 'Its presence is a serious threat. If necessary, I will revert the extra-terrestrial.'

The creature seemed to overhear the chatter and unleashed a bellowing roared in increased agitation. Sound permeated through Joshua's body and settled in the regions of his mind that horded his darkest fears. Every so often, it made a loud bang on the walls that caused slight bends in the metal. He saw The Boogieman was keeping his soul redeemer pointed at the cell at all times. Flanking his left and right were two soul redeemers brandished by other soldiers. Tombstone and the rest of Ghost Team One stood close to The Boogieman ready for action.

'We understand, Colonel,' Hannerman said. 'Hopefully, this will be over quickly. We have a slight problem.'

'Yeah no shit, half my facility's been torn apart,' Marcs replied.

Hannerman released his signature smile. 'Another problem.' He lifted his hand to reveal a circular object constructed of glass except for its metal rim. Energized particles inside the object zipped around with a red glow. 'We have here a storage capsule containing the corrective mind code. However, to administer this code, we'll need to attach it to the specimen's body.'

'That's a lovely, lovely story, doc,' Tombstone said, voice laced with sarcasm.

'Preferably its skull area,' Hannerman said.

Peacemaker laughed. 'Might as well shove it up its ass if you like.'

Another deafening bang on the solid metal wall made the whole floor shake, and the soldiers close to the cell wall backed away from the colonel and the scientists.

'Good luck with that doctor,' Marcs said.

'Unfortunately,' Hannerman said, 'I've had two hip replacements and chronic arthritis.'

'Well so have I doctor,' Marcs said sarcastically. 'No one knew because I was just a lil' shy about it.'

'Your men's athleticism and training make them best suited. All we need is a volunteer.'

'My Asian ass ain't going in there,' Wingman said edging back. 'You could forget that shit.'

Joshua stared at all of the soldiers and sensed that none would volunteer. One out of the crowd pulled his attention. The yellow and dark brown-eyed Black Knight infiltrated his mind. Underneath, a storm must have been brewing, but on the surface one would never know. He just gazed at Joshua, like he was stuck in suspended animation. Yet his jaundice eyes transferred something, a force of energy, and it took over Joshua in a way words could not explain, compelling him to the irrational.

'I'll go!' Joshua said. 'I'll do it.'

He could hear the disappointment in Hannerman's sigh and understandably so. If he were to be injured or killed, Savannah would be lost forever. But the young man saw things differently, this creature, despite its hideous form, could be her, and that seemed to ease his fear. He wasn't the strongest, but he was slender and nimble. After seeing on the cameras how helpless the creature became spinning in zero gravity, he felt the feat attainable.

Peacemaker broke out in unapologetic laughter. 'I see the young buck's nuts have finally dropped.'

Hannerman lowered his tone as he turned to Joshua. 'You sure you want to do this?'

The young man's nerves disabled his voice. Joshua could only nod in reply.

***

Colonel Marcs and Hannerman made their way to the Control Room to monitor the situation via the surveillance system.

Cautiously, Tombstone and Wingman position themselves at either side of the cell door, while Joshua stood in front, hunched in a ready stance, scared out of his mind. The Boogieman kept back, with his soul redeemer at the ready. If he had to use it, with the closeness of their proximities, they could all be dead. Further back was Loca and Peacemaker; the anxious physicist could hear the maniacal soldier laughing.

'Don't worry, doctor' Tombstone said to Joshua, his weapon aimed on the door. 'We've got your back.'

'Better be ready,' Black Knight said, positioning himself.

He replied only with a fearful nod as his limbs tensed, and his adrenaline spiked.

Tombstone counted Joshua down from five—the longest and worst seconds of his life. Black Knight readied to open the door from the control panel. It opened, and a deathly silence welcomed Joshua as he entered the sterile room.

The creature swirled around in mid-air, unable to control itself. To the young man raised in a house of God, the neo-human's hideous form, with its horn-like structures on its head, looked satanic. Its enormity stunned him; just one strike from its powerful arms could break him. Urged forward by the shouts of Ghost Team One, it was difficult to ignore the roar that reverberated through him; at close range the intensity of the chilling sound sent a coldness through every vain in his body. The creature violently kicked and swiped as it floated toward him, but Joshua bobbed and outmaneuvered its attacks. Despite the zero-gravity, the neo-human's power allowed its limbs to generate insanely fast speeds. Joshua knew he wouldn't be able to avoid it for long. Despite the gyroscopes and highly sensitive tilt sensors along the sole of his magnetic boots reacting instantly to his movement, the boot's electromagnetic relays delayed his movement; a delay long enough to get him killed. He ducked another swipe but got caught by the back of its arm. He felt like he had walked into a concrete pillar. Joshua staggered, and the mind code capsule fell out of his hands and floated away from him.

An onrush of pain spread across his face. His vision blurred temporarily, but he made out the black figure getting closer. The soldiers shouted for him to get up quick; he gauged from the intensity of their screams that the creature was in striking distance of him. Another swipe grazed him, ripping his shirt but missing his flesh, causing Joshua to become off-balanced. He stretched his arm the farthest he could in order to grab the capsule, but his high-tech metal boots only allowed him to move one leg off of the ground. Managing to get a few fingers onto the capsule, he immediately dodged another strike. The force the creature exerted on its near-miss caused it to spin, and Joshua seized his moment. He stuck the device onto the back of its hefty skull. The capsule's circulating red particles froze and glowed brighter. Instantly, the creature convulsed then became lifeless and quiet. All five of its eyes closed and it floated tranquilly over the young man. Its limbs curled as it drifted, like the relaxing movement caused by the position of flexion when a bug dies, or a hand goes to sleep.

As the neo-human hovered inches away from his face, its group of eyes soon bolted open and stared at him—close enough for an easy kill.

'Is this a dream?' asked an eerily inhuman, breathless voice. It didn't come from the creature, Joshua felt as though it came from the entire room. Ghost Team One's weapons mirrored the neo-human's movements. Its enlarged head had pupilless eyes filled with a bright red immiscible gas or liquid that dispersed into the air and quickly vanished. 'Are you a dream?' the voice said again, no part of the neo-human's face indicated it was communicating. It merely drifted in its inertial float.

Joshua hesitated to come closer, or even to speak. One swipe of the elongated claws before him could take his head off. He glanced above the neo-human's jagged cranial horns at the speaker in the corner of the ceiling. 'It's using the speaker system to make verbal communication,' Joshua said aloud to inform Hannerman and the others as they listened on the channel.

'It makes sense,' Hannerman's voice on the speaker. 'From our data, they have no properly formed vocal cords. They can only make a limited range of sounds. But they have technopathic abilities.'

'No,' Joshua addressed the neo-human. 'I'm real.'

'Where am I?' said the relayed voice of the creature.

'You are on Earth, well, high above the Earth's surface.'

The creature seemed to lose itself in silence. Uncontrollably it spun on its axis until its oversized head was back in view of him.

'Earth. Can it be?' the creature said. It began to jerk its body and released a shrieking sound. The sound appeared to be random in formation, varying in tone and amplitude, like the sonar of a whale.

'What's happening Joshua?' Hannerman asked on the room's speaker system.

'I think... it's crying.'

'Years I hoped and prayed,' the neo-human said, 'that I would see Earth again. To bathe in the light of its sun.'

Joshua waited a while to make sure the neo-human had finished before speaking. 'My name is Joshua Smith. Do you have a name?'

'I am, Jeremiah...' it's struggled a while to construct its next word. 'Nwakande.'

'Jeremiah, tell me about Olympus, do you remember anything?'

'Olympus...'

'Yes, the other planet.'

'Olympus... I... recall.'

Joshua wasn't quite sure what to say. It was clear that neo-human was in a daze, it must have felt like suddenly waking after being in a year-long coma. He tried to make sure he didn't push Jeremiah. 'What do you recall?'

'The first ones awoke confused, happy to yet still exist, but we longed for Earth, and to understand how we emerged in a strange land. Before the day our minds became inexplicably lost, we existed in a utopia, because we were untethered from the senses of the human body and man's prerequisites of life; to eat, to heal from sickness, to sleep. These necessities and desires kept man busy in a thousand ways. Away from his true purpose and knowledge. On Earth, man's sensory-based existence causes war, tyranny, anarchy, sadness. Our preoccupation with these pursuits kept us from wisdom. On Olympus, we are free of our senses: free of sickness, free of death. Free to love and aspire. With these freedoms, I have witnessed the wonders man can accomplish.'

Joshua found it incredibly difficult to match such human speech to an inhuman image. Nevertheless, despite the fact he knew Moreau would be displeased, he seized the moment he had waited for all along.

'Jeremiah, I'm sorry, but I've lost someone precious to me. She is on Olympus. Her name is Savannah Jenkins. Do you know her?' He hoped that with their telepathic, collective mind-network, the neo-humans might have an awareness of each other.

'I am... sorry. I do not. You love her. You would like to see her again.'

'Yes, desperately; could you help me find her?'

'Whatever you desire, Joshua, I will serve.'

A puzzled frown came upon Joshua's forehead, the word "serve" felt like an odd use of language. But the situation overall was as much of an oddity as you could get.

'Joshua Smith,' called Jeremiah. 'Why did you say, "It's using the speaker system"?'

Joshua was perplexed as to why Jeremiah would ask the question and even more bewildered on how to respond. 'I didn't know you were unable to produce speech.'

'No. Why did you say "it"?'

The young physicist's nerves broke, he stuttered attempting to respond, hoping he hadn't enraged Jeremiah. 'I'm sorry, I'm very sorry, your appearance confused me that's all. But I was wrong to'

'What do you mean... my appearance?'

Joshua was speechless now. At that moment, he saw the neo-human look down at his magnetic boots and observed his own monstrous image in the shiny reflective surface. Immediately Jeremiah went berserk, returning to his animalistic state. 'No!' he cried so loudly it distorted the speakers and forced Joshua to cover his ears from the decibel increase. Jeremiah's words altered, reverting back to a neo-human roar. Thrashing his arms and feet, he began to spin awkwardly. The Ghost Team didn't watch for long, Tombstone and Wingman ventured into the cell and pulled the reluctant Joshua out by his arms and shirt collar. He yelled Jeremiah's name to try and get his attention but to no avail.

CHAPTER SEVEN

THEY WILL DESTROY THEMSELVES

Sometime later, a large number of facility personnel gathered within the Control Room which Joshua hadn't been in since he first came aboard the Ring. It was composed mainly of fighting men and women of the Ghost Teams, recalled on Colonel Marcs' orders. But they weren't just there to defend the Ring, they were prepping for the Olympus incursion. Joshua, Hannerman, Moreau, Colonel Marcs and Tombstone took center stage on the debriefing about the particulars of the mission.

Joshua had a lot going through his mind which made it hard to take in the intricate details being relayed about the planet. He struggled to subdue his thoughts of Jeremiah, who had been left in the detention cell. To ensure his entrapment, the gravity was left off. Joshua wished the Circle of Hermes had allowed him more time to study him, and perhaps unravel some of the neo-human's mystery which might help in his quest for Savannah. He was the only one who seemed to care about Jeremiah's strange behavior. Yet the Circle had denied him any further access to the detention cells.

'There have been further developments on Earth,' Moreau said. Convinced of the experiment's success, he now had a sense of urgency to put boots on the ground on Olympus.

The thought of journeying across an ocean of stars to a world populated by berserk creatures had been less of a concern than solving the problem of teleportation. But now as the time drew imminent, Joshua became terrified of the thought. Yet Moreau's news of Earth had redirected his fears.

The personnel's ambient noise had settled to almost complete silence to Moreau's statement. Their leader, face still dripping with liquid, addressed them.

'The Earth once spun at sixteen hundred kilometers per hour. Its speed has now reduced by three hundred and forty miles per hour, with catastrophic affects.'

'The magnetosphere has weakened,' Hannerman said, surveying the room. 'Solar radiation has become deadly. There have also been mass deaths among populations who had remained near the poles and along the equator due to asphyxiation.'

'The reduced spin created a lack of oxygen,' Joshua said, seeing that some didn't quite understand, the Ghost Teams in particular. 'They suffocated.' He felt his stomach knotting due to the loss of life, along with a sense of responsibility. His inability to solve the matter teleportation problem until now had come at a dire cost. It was ironic, on the surface of the Earth, he had always been nonchalant for these atrocities—Savannah would get annoyed at his lack of empathy. Now far away he had never been so moved. 'What about the UK? What about London?'

'So far,' Hannerman said, 'we're still awaiting detailed reports but most of Europe is being swallowed by a new ocean as we speak. It's only a matter of time for London—'

'The Circle of Hermes have been preparing for this day,' Moreau interrupted. 'Our plans are in motion and are of far greater consequence than the fate of one city... *or* person.'

He was hoping Moreau wouldn't ease up on him since their reality room chat, but Joshua realized that was far too optimistic.

Moreau repeated the ancient words once again. Joshua hadn't forgotten its insidious meaning "*We are power*", and he knew what would happen next. All of the facility's personnel repeated the phase; even the R-MEN that flanked Moreau. It made him cringe, whenever his mind would trick him into believing that this was all just another science project, those haunting words flung him back to a dark reality.

'Now people,' Moreau said with an authoritative, raised voice. 'You know your mission. Colonel Marcs will provide a tactical debrief at 08:00. The mind code must be inserted into the Identifier. No Ghost Team operatives will be permitted back to Earth until the job is done.'

'How many men are you planning to send?' Joshua asked.

'Five teams, sir,' Marcs replied, arms folded like he meant business. Tombstone and his team stood close by to their commanding officer. 'Approximately thirty operators. Ghost Team One will be taking the lead and be in possession of the mind code capsule. That was a cool stunt you pulled Dr. Smith, allowing us to see the neo-humans. Dr. Zahurska is heading up a team of scientists who are rigging up some optical tech that could work in a similar way on our mission.'

It felt odd to Joshua that Zahurska would be chosen to lead the team. Van DeMay was the tech expert and Jonahs had the seniority and authoritative nature. But he had confidence and trust in her to get him to Olympus well-prepared. None of them were present for the briefing, and he found himself missing their newfound team spirit.

'The exoskeletons are ready for deployment, Colonel,' Hannerman said.

'Excellent!' replied Marcs. 'Time to level out the playing field on these sons of bitches.'

Hannerman knew Joshua was unaware of the technology, so he brought him up to speed. 'Each operator will be fitted with an exoskeleton which will enable them to be faster and stronger on Olympus.'

'Excuse me,' Tombstone said. 'Does someone want to explain to me and my team how this teleportation thing is going to work?'

'Yeah,' Wingman said as he brushed his tightly coiled hair with its intricately shaven patterns. 'Because I don't want to turn into wormzilla.'

Black Knight, Loca and The Boogieman looked to Joshua for an explanation. All of the room's personnel followed. He felt Hannerman would have done a better job of a layman's breakdown, still, he obliged.

'So, how do we journey across a trillion miles in a trillionth of a second? The answer lies in how we perceive space.'

'Wait,' Wingman said raising his finger, 'I'm confused.'

'Tonto!' Loca said, rolling her eyes. 'Wing, he just fucking started.'

'Just hold up,' he said, trying to subdue his teammates' chorus of moans. 'Do you mean the space around me, or like stars, quasars and shit?'

'Both,' Joshua replied. 'Space is deemed to be emptiness—what sits in-between things, objects, matter. That space separates objects. This is actually false. Objects are in fact connected across vast distances at the subatomic level, the quantum world. There… nothing is connected, and everything is connected, at the same time.'

Wingman raised his hand again and Joshua addressed him immediately. 'You're still confused, I know.'

Wingman smiled. 'Everyone's fucking confused now. But I get it.'

'You're the biggest dumbass out of all of us,' Loca said shaking her head, 'how you gonna get it?'

'So, Dr. Smith,' Tombstone interrupted, 'how we get to Olympus and back in one piece?'

'First, we make a digitized biological, anatomical copy of your bodies from all levels: starting with a mapping of the brain, then cellular, molecular, atomic. Each stage scales exponentially in difficulties and data processing. Humans are made up of ten to the power of twenty-eight atoms, we'll need to replicate every single one of them to exact precision. The final stage is the quantum level mapping. We then encapsulate the biological data just like we do in data communication, using frames—markers in our case. The higher-level data, i.e. tissue and organs, are encapsulated with markers and passed down to the next layer below, and so forth. At the quantum level, we then entangle the human quantum state with an identical, artificial copy, using Higgs boson particles.'

'Wait, backup,' Tombstone's facial scar morphed as he frowned, focusing on something Joshua had said. 'A copy? You're making copies of us?'

'Yes!' Joshua replied. He saw Tombstone glance over at Wingman and The Boogieman.

'Why is that, homeboy?' Peacemaker asked, his mouth lingered open in a mocking manner.

'Because the original copy is destroyed in the process of teleportation.'

'Destroyed? You're joking, right?' Tombstone said. For a composed man, he looked close to losing it.

'Man, this is some bullshit,' Wingman said turning himself away. 'Black was right, Sarge, from the moment we met this guy fucked up shit just keeps happening…'

'Secure that mouth of yours, Trooper!' Marcs ordered.

'You're not destroying my body, little man,' The Boogieman said in one of the deepest voices Joshua had ever heard. It was also the first time he had heard the gigantic man speak.

Joshua continued. 'Everyone who will be teleported—they will cease to exist, and a new, identical version of you must be created.'

'Is that necessary, señor?' Loca asked. The Black Knight stood silently by her side, firing laser beams of animosity with his gaze.

'Absolutely necessary.'

'Doctor,' Tombstone said. 'How do we know that this identical version of me will be the same as who I am now? Why don't you just send the original, genuine me?'

'We can't just send the original copy because in the quantum world, when you observe something, you automatically change what it is. If we were to interact with and transmit our quantum selves directly, when you get to the other side, you will be completely different; diametrically different, different in ways I fear to comprehend. Now, picture three particles; particle A which represents you, particle B, which is located on Earth and it is entangled with particle C, which resides on Olympus. If we take particle A, you, and make particle B a mirror copy of A, and then measure the quantum states of particle A and B together, by doing so particle C's state on Olympus will instantaneously become A's state. That's how the teleportation works. The process of quantumizing your body and measuring its state means that as soon as we scan and analyze your quantum state, it is immediately altered or destroyed. But the copy retains all your information.'

'Ok now you lost me again, dude,' Wingman said.

Tombstone pointed a stern finger at Joshua. 'You better just make sure I get back to Earth as pretty as I left doctor.'

'That's the idea, Mr. Tombstone,' Hannerman said. 'Colonel, we would need to quantumize everything that's being teleported, weapons and ammunition too.'

'Affirmative!' Marcs said. 'So, once my boys arrive on Olympus, how do we put these humpty dumpties back together again and bring them back?'

'That part is much less complicated,' Hannerman replied.

'Matter and energy are related and therefore can be converted. All we need is Higgs particles and ultrafaron for its energy transducing properties. The planet is full of both. We will establish a gateway at a predetermined location for exfiltration, which we called the focal point. We also need to administer injections to all incursion operatives.'

'Why do we need injections?' Peacemaker asked. He had a hint of nonchalant arrogance in his voice.

Wingman came close to Peacemaker to whisper in his ears. 'You already got AIDS crackerjack; no shot can save you.'

Hannerman responded. 'The gravity of Olympus is four times that of Earth. Injection one will strengthen your skeletal structure. The second is an accelerating steroid that will boost your muscle strength. The third shot will hyper-increase your blood pressure and supercharge your heart so that it can keep pumping blood around your body. Without the shots, you wouldn't last very long.'

'So, when do we leave?' Joshua asked.

'We?' Peacemaker said. 'The fuck do you think you're going? This isn't a scientific expedition.'

'You've got big balls, man,' Loca said. Nodding in admiration. 'Big hairy balls.'

'Maybe,' Wingman remarked, smiling as he stared at Joshua's slim, unimposing physique, 'but his arms don't look like they've ever seen a dumbbell.'

'I need to be there.'

Peacemaker came right in. 'I'll tell you what homeboy, if we find any cool bacteria out there, we'll radio it in!'

'Oh, I'm going, whether you—'

'That will not be necessary,' Moreau said.

'I need to make sure I get Savannah back,' Joshua said, enraged.

'Who?' said Marcs and his executive officer next to him simultaneously, completely bewildered.

'Your presence will not be required, Smith,' Moreau said. 'Ghost Teams have been assigned to find her after they complete their objective, if it is possible. If they find her, they will capture her and bring her back.'

'That's not good enough!' Joshua shouted. 'Their primary objective is their mission, inserting the corrective code into the Identifier. As soon as they've done that, *my* concerns will matter little.'

'Dr. Smith,' Tombstone said. His words were uttered peacefully compared to his colleagues' aggressive tones. 'I'm sorry it had to be this way. But our mission is against all odds as it is. We're going to have the weight of one hundred and fifty million hostiles concentrated on us. Trust me, you don't want to be there.'

'You're not going without me and that's that.'

'Thank you for your assistance thus far, doctor,' Colonel Marcs said, lacking all emotion. 'You will have to bench this one out. A security detail will escort you to your quarters. Dr. Hannerman will update you on our progress as and when he can. You have my word.'

Joshua saw two soldiers animate as if they had waited to execute orders already given to them. 'You still need me to operate the Transcender,' he shouted as he felt the forceful grip of hands all over him.

'My people should be able to handle things from here,' Moreau said.

The two guards began to drag Joshua towards the entrance doors kicking and squirming as he screamed 'You can't do this!'

'Excellent work, Dr. Smith,' Colonel Marcs said as the physicist struggled to free himself. 'You will be a hero. Although the world will never know.'

LAYERED VISION

The Mind-Body Problem

CHAPTER EIGHT

TO KNOW SUFFERING

Hours passed. Joshua sat in silence and solitude in his quarters, which now functioned as his prison cell. He tried for hours to pry the doors open, and screamed to the guards to release him, but to no avail.

It was nearly 6am GMT, still at least two hours before Moreau had said the tactical debrief would begin, which meant the incursion hadn't gone ahead yet. Despite the slim odds, he still had hope of making it to Olympus, if he could only escape what had now become his cell.

Brute force had little effect, so he unlocked his GCD to try to find a way to hack the door controls. As he executed different commands, the doors parted open. It was easier than he thought— so he thought. He made three steps to the door before abruptly stopping at the sight of one R-MEN robot consuming the door frame. Its six-foot-four inches metal and polycarbonate body forced him back by its presence alone. All the robot did was stare at him with eyes which were designed, before their uprising, to elicit tranquility and trust.

'Excuse me,' said a familiar voice.

The robot provided a monotoned, yet kind, apology and backed away. Dr. Hannerman walked in and the doors slid shut quickly behind him.

'You lied to me!' said the angered young physicist. 'The

uncertainty principle wasn't what corrupted the Olympians. Admit it.'

Hannerman simply nodded his head in shame.

'I'm surprised it took me so long to figure it out. The Circle caused the neo-humans to go berserk. You corrupted their minds in a failed attempt to rule over them in Olympus like gods. Everything became clear after seeing how Jeremiah's mind eventually turned subservient as the corrective code took over him.'

Hannerman delayed responding, then unleashed a dual smile and frown, as though trying to hide his own disappointment. The weight of his thoughts forced him to take a seat. 'For over three hundred years, scientists and philosophers have argued over whether the human conscious exists as a separate entity to the body, or if it's simply a part of the human body; with effectively the mind being merely an outcome of biochemistry too complex to be understood.'

'The mind-body problem,' Joshua interrupted. 'That is trivial, you solved that already. The neo-humans exist—the mind is not connected to the body.'

'The first neo-human ever formed, the one that came through the Transcender we told you about. Once he realized what he was, within a few moments, he went insane. He tore the place apart before fleeing back through to Olympus. We never solved the mind-body problem. Think about it. The soul could have reconstituted itself into any possible form, but what it chose was humanoid: bipedal symmetry etcetera, etcetera. Every single one of them.'

'The Higgs particles didn't just infuse into their mind, but their bodies as well. It must have created a residual anthropomorphic blueprint. What's your point?'

'I believe that the soul is inexorably linked to the body. Therefore, even if neo-humans could have survived instant mental collapse, they would have sought to recreate their old, human image eventually. Who knows how long that could take them, decades? Centuries? Never? But until they could accomplish that, it was possible, even if unlikely *still... possible*, that they could have fallen into a terminal cycle because they would have hated their new physical form, since they would still be conscious of their original form. Thus, spiraling into a state of manic depression and hatred, which could lead to their own self-destruction.'

'Ah come on! That is so disputable it's ridiculous. That you would even think to proceed with consequential actions based on such a flimsy hypothesis.' More passion than anger erupted from Joshua now. 'I can just sense Moreau and the influence of his social degeneration theories. How could you be so sure? They would have most likely overcome their appearance. You can change the frame of a portrait, but the picture remains the same. Irrespective of the construct that forms the vessel of our souls, are we not still men? Endowed with the potential of morality and nobility?'

'Joshua for goodness sake, you are a theoretical physicist, but I'm asking you now to be practical, to be rational.'

'Rational? When was the last world war, doctor? When was the last empire forged in blood on a battlefield? Long ago, mankind had learned to overcome their hatred—not totally but substantially to coexist. Reason and rationale overpowered hatred before, and it would have done so again.'

'No, no, no, what you're referring to is hatred for one another, what I'm talking about is hatred for oneself. On a societal scale; man has never fought that battle. If you don't believe me, ask yourself the question, and answer it aloud. When you first laid eyes on that neo-human we captured, what thoughts came into your mind when you looked at him?'

Joshua's body went limp, his anger levels dropped. He didn't want to answer the question, but truth compelled him. 'Monster!' he said, knowing the old man had a point. 'Satanic Monster.'

'A healthy sense of vanity is pivotal to our existence. It is impossible to be positive and fulfilled in life, *and* hate oneself. Even worse, that you've become the stuff not of dreams but of nightmares and mythological horror. Then there are those who are still secretly religious—who have their own beliefs of the afterlife, of existence. Only now for their reflection to become their own personifications of evil. Add all of this to the misery of no longer being able to engage in man's desires, to… to… to be unable to be intimate with the woman you love, yearn for the taste of a good home-cooked meal. Neo-human bodies do not have these senses. When I amplified that trauma and negative, individual self-image by the magnitude of a society's population, every result in my simulation's predictions were the same—catastrophic!' Hannerman composed himself with a few deep breaths, realizing he had gotten caught up in his argument. 'You saw Jeremiah's reaction yourself when he saw his reflection. An ugly duckling needs to know, or in this case be led to believe, it is a swan.'

'So, you brainwashed them.'

The old man's wrinkled face twisted and contorted as he struggled to accept the statement. 'I gave them the neuroscientific equivalent of a... hypnotic suggestion.'

'So the Circle of Hermes made you wipe the image of the human form from the souls of the transcended.'

Hannerman agreed with a nod. 'But, unbeknownst to me, the Circle ordered Moreau to manipulate my coding for control. By the time I found out there was little I could do. I felt it best to hide the crimes from you because of my shame, but also because the more you knew Joshua, the more of a threat you are to the Circle of Hermes; they may have never allowed you to leave the Ring if you weren't fully on board with the project, and I wasn't sure if you would be.'

Joshua walked around the room to calm himself. After a moment to think about things, Joshua spoke again. 'The Circle never intended on saving the millions of Unknowns or Savannah, only to cure the corruption and assert their control, so that Olympus will once again be their physical heaven, one that they can rule over. They've been manipulating and corrupting

LAYERED VISION

Social Degeneration

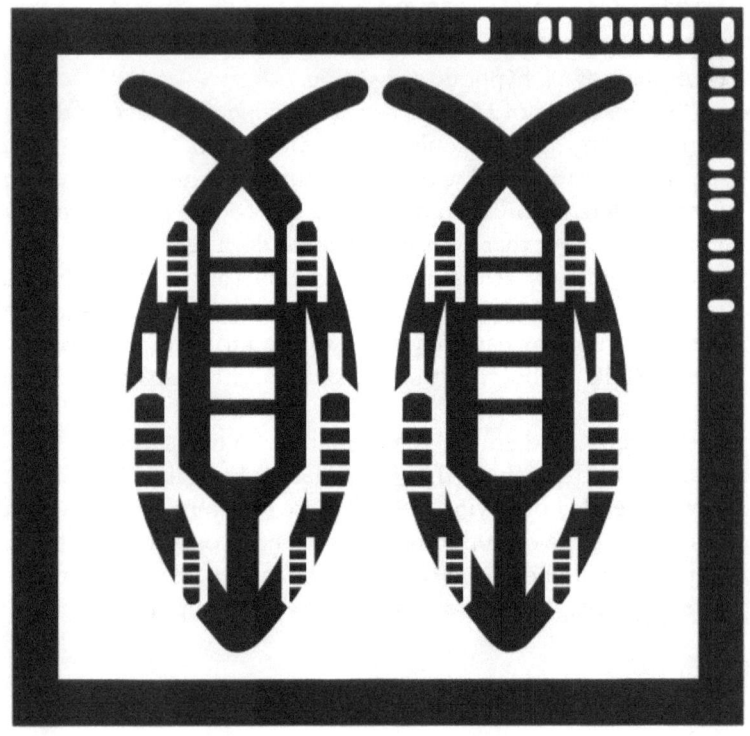

you from the beginning, Frank. I know that for you, it was about preserving our essence, but for the Circle it was always about power.'

'You never cared until you lost what was precious to you. I cared until I lost what *was* precious to me. When she left, the best of me left with her. Everything mattered less after that. Now that they know that this version of the mind code restores knowledge of their former image, Moreau will modify it so that it doesn't.'

Joshua went and placed his hand on Hannerman's shoulders.

'Socrates said that all wrongdoing is the result of ignorance. Open your eyes to the truth; you proved that the soul is eternal, and if it is then it will endure, even if Olympus doesn't. We... harness our knowledge in order to attempt to better the world but let he who would move the world first move himself. Please Frank, help me get to Olympus before it's too late.'

'Joshua, what can I do? I'm just an old man, out of touch with the world.'

'Do something. Moreau, he looks weak...'

'Moreau is far older, and far more dangerous than you can possibly imagine.'

'What do you mean?'

'The initial project to extend human life. Look, it doesn't matter. No one can stop the Circle's plans. I'm sorry my dear friend.'

***

A few hours had passed. Joshua sat once more, contemplating fate itself. Hannerman had been summoned by Moreau to meet him at the Quantum Room as the mission was about to commence. In his solitude, he thought about the countless lives lost when the Ring activated and the Earth slowed even further. He had willfully played a part in that, for the sake of his own loss. His hypocrisy gnawed at him; his morality fared no better than Hannerman's as he now attempted to fight for what was lost to him. He felt his hope of ever seeing Savannah again painfully slip away.

Unexpectedly, the room doors opened. This time, to Joshua's surprise, the Black Knight stepped in. In the darkness of the room, Joshua could barely see his face, but his cold yellowish eyes radiated with an ominous intent.

'If I remember the story correctly,' Black Knight said, stepping closer, 'Ebenezer Scrooge was visited by three ghosts before Christmas.'

'Christmas! So, you're a believer of the birth of Christ now, Mr. Black Knight?'

'What do you know about *belief*, Smith? Now that they know your true feelings, the Circle of Hermes will never let you live, not unless you serve them, forever a prisoner in these cursed walls.'

'They're going to need my help soon or later, otherwise, I'd be dead already.'

'All those scientists that surrounded you, when you forged your blasphemous creation, were these infidels merely in awe of your greatness? Or serving their truer purpose? Carefully detailing and recording your work. Intellectual ego, the fatal flaw of all men of science.'

The soldier's words were like a bat to Joshua's face. In his ignorance and tragedy, he did not conceive that he would be betrayed by Zahurska and Van DeMay, less so of Jonahs. He felt that he been fooled, because he was a fool. Hannerman was right about him not thinking clearly. Now, he was no longer needed and in serious trouble.

'Right now, all I really care about is tracking down the host body with my partner's soul so I can bring her out of her coma.'

'You serve purely your own gains. As you have done since the tragedy of your mother.'

'How do you know about…'

'You have been lost ever since, brother,' Black Knight said.

'Who are you? Who are you really?'

'Who am I? I am a true knight.'

'*You made me bold with strength; in my soul*—these were your words while you were being attacked by the creature—Jeremiah. It was almost unintelligible over the speakers, except for someone who has heard the bible passage recited countless times. You're a man of faith.'

'I am a sword of an order that has existed since the ancient times, established by all those that believe in the one true God. Followers of Mohammed, Abraham and Christ unite under us.'

'The group behind the terrorist attack? The Builders… of Jericho? You're one of them.'

'They think they are legion, but the Circle's power is frail compared to our own, which in itself is feeble compared to him the creator. We built the pyramids, forged the knights Templar; God gave man morality, but we enforced it. We protect what is precious, and to ensure his children reach the gates of heaven, I would gladly fight in hell for all eternity. Both the righteous and the condemned—the souls of man must go to where they rightfully belong. Our knights have created our own mind code, a neural bomb designed to destroy the neurological pathways of all the demons. Once I insert it into the Identifier, it will bring an end to both the extragalactic hell and your sacrilegious science. And like scriptures told centuries ago, our knights will topple the Towers of Babel, so all souls will be judged once more.'

'Hold up. I agree with you, just wait for me to find my fiancé first. Her soul's been taken as a result of my work. It's my fault.'

'Now you see it is your fault.'

'If she died naturally I could deal with it; but she was taken unnaturally.'

'I care nothing for your woman, only for His world.'

'Well, she's my world,' Joshua yelled as desperation settled in.

'What sense is it, brother, for a man to destroy a whole world to save himself?'

'Look, once I get her back, I can help—'

'I do not need your help, betrayer of God!' The Black Knight spewed out savagely through his teeth. 'I may come as one, but I stand as millions.'

'Listen to me. I can repair the entanglement of Earth and Olympus and find a way to kick the Earth back to a faster rotation which will eventually stop the natural disasters. I will help you destroy the teleportation machine.'

'Blasphemer, you are unfit to aid me. A lost mind can never survive in God's army. I need not wish your demise, a poisoned mind in time destroys its own body. Evil triumphs when good men do nothing. What have you been doing all this time?'

'I've been selfish in the past, I know that—neglected everyone who cared about me. Savannah, my dad. For that neglect I'm suffering, and my pain won't go away until I get her back. For crying out loud, I've got less than forty-eight hours, help me. I'm begging you, please.'

'It's too late.'

'It's not—'

'It's too late!' Black Knight shouted. 'An earthquake has hit East London. It's knocked out all power to the Homerton Hospital, including backup generators and communication. Everyone requiring life support could not survive—the Hive is gone.'

'No! There—'

'The Unknowns there are no more.' The soldiers' words were uttered without even a fraction of empathy.

Joshua's face drooped, like he suffered a stroke. 'I've... lost her... truly lost her. My suffering has only just begun.'

For a moment, the soldier only looked at Joshua, not saying a word. After an uncomfortable silence, he gave Joshua his reply.

'I was born in the heart of the Congo and brought to England when I was ten years old.' His buried African accent emerged. 'A militia raped and killed my sister and mother. Cut off both arms and legs of my father and brothers, and then ate the rest of them in front of me. I was only five at the time.'

Black Knight moved closer to Joshua, but the intensity in his eyes compelled the smaller black male to step back towards the wall more and more.

'They took me and made me a boy soldier in the liberation army. I killed hundreds of men before I was even a man. I was forced to rape. They made me drink the blood of my victims, told me it would grant me power and immortality. One day, another rebel group captured and tortured me. They pulled my teeth out with pliers and were going to kill me. But I was rescued.'

Like a Trapdoor spider pouncing upon its prey, the soldier grabbed Joshua by his neck with both his hands and the physicist felt what seemed like extraordinary strength. It might as well be The Boogieman that gripped him. Slowly his life drained from his body and he was powerless to stop it.

'What do you know of pain, Smith? What do you understand of suffering? The demon will come for you, brother. Be ready to greet · it.'

The soldier released his chokehold, much to Joshua's grasping relief. He stormed his way to the entrance door, and it opened automatically. The RM-V9 series unit stood ominously in the doorway. Blue artificial eyes scanned the scene; witnessing Joshua gripping his bruised neck on the ground before looking back at the black soldier.

'Smith is to speak to no one,' Black Knight ordered the R-MEN in rage, 'and allowed no other visitors until the mission on Olympus is complete. Do you understand?'

There were a few silent seconds before the R-MEN finished processing a reply.

'As you wish.'

CHAPTER NINE

ACROSS AN OCEAN OF STARS

Zahurska, Van DeMay and Jonahs headed up the multiple scientists that scurried like foraging bugs around the grand teleportation machine. The Quantum Room was overfilled largely by Ghost Teams who congregated within their respective units—all loaded up in tactical gear. Black Knight spent much of his time in silence gazing at the robotic exoskeleton he wore with a displeasing frown. His Ghost Team clothing was still visible for the most part, but now a silver, metal frame covered the major skeletal sections of his body. Wearing the exoskeleton, he felt like he could run straight through a solid wall. Staring at Moreau standing with his robotic guards, ordering Ring personnel around, his urges attempted to persuade him that the advanced combat suit was all the power he needed to topple the Circle once and for all. His head spun, trying to fully recover from the side effects of the Olympus injections; most of the soldiers experienced a lingering acute pain from involuntary muscle contractions. The injection to their spines sent pulses of agony through their entire bodies and their joints had seized up momentarily. But the shot to Black Knight's heart had it pumping like a canon.

He watched The Boogieman coming toward him, he had just lifted a transportation container containing mobile base stations onto the Transcender's platform, shifting the hundred kilograms with ease. The Boogieman stared back at him; few words had been shared between them since he had saved the muscular man's life on a previous mission. The big man had it in his mind that Black Knight was something, something that wasn't quite human. The African soldier had tried a few times to make conversation with him, but The Boogieman had made it obvious without words that he preferred to keep away from him. The last words the giant said to him was that he owed him is life.

Peacemaker threw forceful punches in the air that drew Black Knight's attention; his exoskeleton made a mechanical noise of alternating pitch with each strike. 'Hey boy,' said the deranged man in a deep south swagger to Black Knight when he noticed his gaze. 'What say we go a few rounds when I get back, June bug.' His pupils were bright red thanks to the optical implants all Ghost Teams were given. Though the nanotech would help them to visualize the neo-humans, it gave their eyes a sinister red glow in dim light.

'Don't be so sure you'll be coming back,' Black Knight replied.

'If I don't, neither will you.' With the exoskeleton's protective helmet covering Peacemaker's unkempt hair, he looked like a killer cyborg. 'You think you're fooling everyone with this Zen yoga silent shit. Negro please! Lyin' like a no-legged dog! Remember, I've seen the real you. The you that you try to hide in that sewage pipe you call a soul. You didn't think I would forget, did you? All of those innocent bodies in Germany stacked up around us! The Sarge thinks you ain't never been the same since the insurrection. But I know the truth... you're as much of a monster as me.'

Black Knight had lost his words. Instead of his usual blank expression, micro twitches barely detectable to the untrained eye made Peacemaker laugh sadistically.

A small aerial drone dropped in front of Black Knight like a spider dropping from its web. It hovered head-height and beamed a red laser at his eyes. Instinctively he cocked his hand back to launch a punch.

'No!' Van DeMay cried out from a distance away. 'It just wants to install the optic enhancers on to your pupils. 'It won't hurt.'

'I can hunt them without seeing them.'

'Let him be,' said Dr. Jonahs. He was an arm's length from Van DeMay, directing the drones to each Ghost Team operator.

'Yo Peacemaker!' Wingman said, waving a short, metal staff in the air like he was swatting flies. One swipe forced the short Loca to duck and unleash a barrage of Spanish expletives. 'I can just imagine how many little boys you would *love* to abuse with this.' Each time he swung, neon blue lights illuminated the staff and dissipated when the motion stopped.

'Or I could shove it up your vagina,' said the badly groomed soldier.

'Mr. Wingman,' Hannerman said, raising protesting open hands. 'Please, do not swing that baton. We've upgraded the standard law enforcement microwave nightstick into a Higgs frequency disruptor.'

Wingman flipped the baton like a juggling stick. 'You know doc, that's exactly what I thought it was—a Higgency Dissarutter.'

'Correct,' Hannerman said not wanting to waste time with an explanation. 'It won't kill the neo-humans, but it should inflict heavy damage on them.' Hannerman raised his voice to get all the infiltration teams' attention. 'If you noticed on the left arm of your exoskeleton there is a metal armband. It's what keeps your exosuit's battery pack charged, but it can become dangerous if destabilized so, protect it with your life. I repeat—do not damage your powerbands.'

'Dr. Hannerman,' Moreau said, raising his voice from across the room. 'It is time.' Moreau turned to the augmented reality display of the Control Room and everyone had formed a circle around the projection. Military personnel filled the AR display, with Colonel Marcs front and center. 'We are ready, Colonel.'

'Ghost Teams, listen up,' Marcs said. His voice came across the loudspeakers as he remained in the facility's control room where he would be commanding the operation. 'The machine is ready. We will perform the first ever human teleportation across the universe. Your theatre of operations will be completely unfamiliar territory. But you will have no time for sightseeing when you're on the other side. Stay focused on the objectives. Remember, the focal point will drop you in within thirty kilometers of the target location. Good luck! Waiting for your command, Mr. Moreau.'

Moreau panned across the faces of the fighting men with the sternest of gazes. 'For centuries we have conquered life; now we will conquer death.'

'We are power!' said the room full of personnel.

'Do not fail,' Moreau said.

The Ghost Teams ready themselves with last minute checks of

their gear and supplies.

'Thirty klicks through a neo-human nightmare,' Loca whispered to Black Knight. She only vocalized what the minds of all the soldiers were thinking. Despite their upgraded tech, the odds of survival stacked against them. 'The place is going to be crawling with hostiles.'

'Stay close,' Black Knight said to her.

'Your spider-senses itching again, Caballero?' she said. Loca kept her focus on her weapons check and looked relieved by the exoskeleton's pneumatics assistance of MKEPX13's weight.

'This isn't going to end well, for any of us.'

'Hey look, we do this right—no more reversion missions. We go back to doing easy work, squashing anti-charter uprisings and shit.'

'There won't be anything to go back to, Loca.'

She grabbed his exosuit's chest plate and yanked him forward. 'Then the Circle will give us a pass to Olympus if we're successful. Now drop this shit, Caballero—and do your job.' She both shouted and yet whispered her words through her teeth so they wouldn't be overheard.

He found himself speechless when she came too close, she stirred up the emotions that life had robbed him of feeling. The Builders of Jericho had told him he was ordained for a great purpose, and his journey along his path had made him a Knight of bloodshed. Yet in her eyes, he saw a different visual of himself—and she noticed it too.

'It's time, Ghost Team One,' Tombstone ordered. He led the team onto the teleportation platform. 'Canine units assigned to Ghost Team One, move out.'

Following them were two, four-legged robots with body frames similar to a large dog, but greater in size. One robot had a twin MKEPX13 rifle while a bulky soul redeemer fashioned to the back of the other.

Black Knight watched the silver coils that lay under the transparent floor spark with energy. He stepped onto the circular platform, The Boogieman on one side and Tombstone on the other. He raised his eyes to the ceiling and shook his head at the sight of the ominous metal arm above.

'Ghost Team One, come in,' Colonel Marcs said on their radio link.

'We read you, Colonel,' Tombstone said.

'I will monitor operations from the control room. Once you confirm successful teleportation, the other teams will follow. Is that Understood GT1?'

'Sir, yes sir,' the team said.

'So, if our brains don't explode, they'll know that it worked,' Peacemaker said.

'First in, GT One,' Tombstone said.

'Last out!' the team replied.

'Activate the Transcender, Dr. Zahurska,' Hannerman said.

Zahurska now assumed Joshua's position, leading Van DeMay and Jonahs through the initialization sequence with a confidence of authority that hadn't existed in Joshua's presence.

Powerful electrical crackles and bangs made Ghost Team One jittery as the Transcender came to life with light. Before long, they were trapped by the power of magnetism. Ghost Team One were lifted into the air. The blue orb engulfed them, and sensations Black Knight had never comprehended bombarded his mind. His eyes were opened but he couldn't interpret the visuals he saw. His thoughts were suspended in reality for a moment. He had one notion before it all became a blur—he would no longer exist. Who he will become would be an imposter, a malignant reflection. But for the sake of what he believed in he had to stay true to who he was. If he could do that through the hellish storm, he would not lose himself.

After the orb expanded, they vanished.

All they felt was that a split second of time had passed; all they saw…was purple.

After the blinding white light vanished, the armed team discovered that they had materialized on black earth. Barely a moment in time had passed, but they had travelled across literally a quadrillion stars. Immediately they all dropped to the floor due to weakness and nausea. Except for The Boogieman—the six-foot eleven inches black soldier's legs and center mass grounded him upright.

Despite Black Knight's injections and enhancements, his organs struggled to adjust to the gravity which was four times that of Earth's. His hand slammed on the planet's dark surface. His head was a windmill of spinning unstructured images. He felt the ultrafaron earth was smoother than marble, more polished than rocks on a shoreline worn smooth by wave and sand. Its surface had been artificially laid by the land's inhabitants.

Fighting back their disorientation, they looked to the sky and saw an awe-inspiring sight before them.

'Olympus,' Tombstone said, with a wide-opened mouth. He breathed in deep, trying to force more air into his battered lungs.

They had a full view of a city before them. In the distance, lay miles upon miles of pointed buildings, constructed at a sixty-five-degree angle. The structures resembled a multitude of slim-line pyramids forged of a shimmering dark mauve and gold, stretching further into the atmosphere than the tallest of Earth's skyscrapers. But the view was not the utopia that they had prepared for in their combat simulations. Most of the structures laid in ruin; more abundant than the slanted pyramids was an uneven terrain of rubble that once made up the majestic architecture of this higher civilization. What remained standing was destroyed beyond repair; sections of their composition stripped or blasted out down to its inner frame, giant cracks covered every inch of surface. It was the type of damage a mega-earthquake would cause, or the detonation of a nuclear bomb.

'So, this shithole is heaven?' said Peacemaker shaking off his dizziness.

'No,' Black Knight scowled at the scene. 'It's just a shithole.' The reason why the neo-human they captured mentioned that he had longed for Earth's light was evident. No star's rays could penetrate this purple sky thick with plumes of grayish mist obscuring the land, merging high above into a blanket of magenta clouds. 'Khufu would've been amazed.'

'Ku who?' asked Tombstone.

'He was the pharaoh who built the great pyramid,' Black Knight replied.

'They've destroyed what they've built,' Loca said, 'in their madness. Que puto día!'

While the rest were dumbstruck, Wingman looked around anxiously at the broken terrain of black rock. 'No sign of hostiles. But we're sitting ducks out here, man. We need to move.'

'Not yet, Trooper,' Tombstone said. 'Loca, help me get the mobile base station link established with the Ring. Peacemaker— do a status check on the canines, confirm they're in recon mode. I don't want them giving away our position. Everyone else, secure a perimeter. Don't let these fuckers sneak up on us.'

Loca stooped low next to a weighty metal case that had been teleported with them. After a few presses of its LCD screen, it automatically opened. A multi-antenna device rose up as if commanded, unfolding itself in mechanical motor churns. It grew larger before their eyes until it reached a meter tall.

Meanwhile, Peacemaker's nostrils became pink with the rush of blood as he continuously sniffed the air. 'Smells like the ass of my last whore,' he said, before spitting out some phlegm.

'There's a high concentration of ammonia in the air,' Loca said, her tablet's sensors had confirmed the readings they had prepped for.

'How long before that comms link is up, L?' Wingman asked her, uncomfortable in his new surroundings. Being exposed in the open played on his nerves. He shoved his hand between his exoskeleton's abdominal protective plating and held his stomach in discomfort. 'Fucking drugs, man. Diarrhea is going to kill me before the monster-men do.'

'You've always been full of shit,' Peacemaker said.

'Shit ain't funny, man.'

'Over there,' Black Knight said, pointing at a sideward angle. 'That's where the Identifier will be.'

Far in the distance through the grayish-purple mist-plumes, they saw a monument, the only grand structure that still stood pristine in the dire panoramic. Foreboding clouds encircled it like they were being swirled with a giant rod held by divine hands. It was over a mile in height; two giant serpents wrapped around a giant winged tower, just like the emblem of the Circle of Hermes.

***

Joshua laid on his hard bed, struggling with the rush of depression that fed off of his hopelessness. His throat throbbed, sore from his constant yelling to be freed; the pain in his neck from Black Knight's gripped lingered as though it would never dissipate. Hours passed, no one came. He doubted if he would even see much of Hannerman again. His failure was complete, Savannah was lost to him for good. He wondered if by now, the Circle had already inserted the mind code; or if Black Knight could have succeeded in his intent to sabotage the Illuminati's fiendish plans.

His mind had stopped plotting ways to escape his prison; his fists, bruised from banging on the walls. His once unstoppable will had given up.

'GCD,' Joshua said. 'Load up previous video recordings of Savannah.'

'They are thirty-seven video files in my storage that captures at least a minute of Savannah's presence,' the genius device said in a tranquil tone. 'Please specify which file—'

'Just play any one of them.'

'Ok Joshua. One moment.'

Savannah appeared within his quarters again and stood motionless in front of him in her aform.

'No GCD, pause playback. Wait.' Hearing her voice would have only caused his mind to spiral. He reached out to touch her, but his hand went through her face. Multiple micro-haptic sensors embedded within small pads in his hand provided a sensation of contact with her, using electrical signals, force, vibration and motion. But it was merely a sophisticated mirage, creating a ghost which he realized now would only serve to haunt him forever.

'Don't play anything. Turn it off.'

'Okay,' said the passive male voice. 'As you wish.'

Like a true mirage, she vanished. The real Savannah remained in the Unknown Hive; the real Savannah—was dead. He would have to come to terms with it, never getting a chance to say goodbye. A life where every second without her would feel like decades and to wonder if time could one day make her fade from his mind for good. He recalled the parents that he saw in the hive, sobbing inconsolably at their young daughter's bedside. Perhaps he had been spared the same fate.

A thought occurred to him in the depths of his despair, one that had never crossed his mind since his adolescence; one that he swore to himself he would bury forever. He sat up at the edge of the bed, contemplating why he had not screamed out in objection to the notion that festered in his mind. The last time he carried out these acts was the last time he heard his mother's voice. Joshua dropped down to his knees and folded his fingers into each other, before closing his eyes.

'Father, I have sinned against heaven and against you. I am no longer worthy to be called your son. Help me Father, I know... I cannot save her, only you can giveth life to the dead, and calleth the things that are not, as though they were. So, I leave Savannah and my mother in your merciful hands and ask you to grant me the serenity to accept the things I cannot change, the courage to change the things I can, and the wisdom to know the difference.'

Soon after, he heard commotion and screams coming from outside his room, then the unmistakable sound of gunfire. The sounds of chaos drew nearer and intensified, causing his limbs to tremble as he moved further away from the door. As his heart raced, he remembered Black Knight's words "There were three ghosts before Christmas".

Hannerman was the first, the soldier was the second. The third ghost now approached him.

***

The Ring received Ghost Team One's communication, their report of the ruined landscape shocked the Circle's personnel, Moreau in particular. They had all envisioned Olympus to be unchanged from the footage stored within their multitude of server clusters—as an extra-terrestrial paradise, not a wasteland.

Marcs ordered the other four Ghost Teams to proceed to Olympus after Tombstone had confirmed their location was secure. Ghost Team One ran point, doing reconnaissance for the mission as each Ghost Team performed overwatch maneuvers on the broken terrain; switching from forward movement to providing cover. They looked like a trail of ants in the land of the giants, seeking cover between the damaged, black, alien structures. Almost tripping, Wingman's mouth couldn't close as he angled his rifle up to the rows of majestic floating towers. The outer surface of the towers were a fusion of advance technology and ancient glyphs; most were releasing pillars of smoke.

They had yet to detect any neo-humans, and the more ground they covered provided a sense of ease, even hope that their mission might be without casualties. Perhaps the new humans had left for a more distant part of the planet. Some of the operators felt confident that they must have perished, there was a growing belief that the neo-humans in their mentally unstable state, would eventually degenerate back into the ultrafaron soil, losing all corporeal form.

Olympus' seemingly desolate pyramids made the perfect

ambush points; so vast and numerous, it would have taken them years to search every crevice inside their inscribed walls, even with triple their Ghost Team numbers. The megastructures and the planet's mist, with its forever-shifting levels of opacity, compelled the Ghost Teams to never drop their guards. They ordered their robotic canine units to form a defensive perimeter; the ten titanium-alloy, four-legged drones maneuvered the difficult terrain with ease. Along with standard motion detectors, canine drones were programmed to use their microelectromechanical systems to detect variances in heat. This was mainly to avoid them firing on the teams as the neo-humans' heat signatures were barely detectable. At times, the drone dogs turned and remained focused in a direction, analyzing something that took their interest. Each of these occurrences caused a mini panic amongst Ghost Teams.

'I've got movement,' Loca said, focusing on her tablet-size GCD. The team ducked low in response.

'Where are they?' Tombstone asked. His raised fist signaled to the other teams to halt.

They waited in silence against the howling wind that blew fine, black particles in their faces. Tension built up in their muscles, blood rushed through their limbs as the fight or flight responses kicked in like never before.

'I think they're up ahead,' Loca replied with a lack of certainty that made her team anxious.

'Range?' Tombstone said.

'They're all over the place, jefe.'

'I don't see shit,' Peacemaker said. He squinted his eyes, desperate for his vision to cut through the mist and the giant, fallen sections of the neo-human's buildings.

'We need a visual,' Tombstone said. 'Wingman, inform the other teams.'

'Whatever I'm picking up,' Loca said, 'UAV six is almost in range. I'm loading up live stream now.'

'Yeah pretty please, L,' Wingman said, his forearm shaking. 'That'll be nice.'

'Shut up!' Loca replied.

An image of a congregation of neo-humans projected in the air, distorted into grainy footage by the alien atmosphere. The display cycled through different viewpoints, zoom levels and adjustments in angles; feeding back textual data. It then cycled through more groups of neo-humans the drones had detected.

Tombstone uttered a word in Polish that conveyed his shock. 'There must be close to a thousand of them.'

They were used to hunting lone hostiles and had hoped for a non-combat stealth mission; what they dreaded was a war. That felt like a probable outcome as they watched the swarm of new humans moving in a stiff, slow, uncoordinated manner.

'Do they remind you of something?' Wingman said.

'Yeah,' Peacemaker replied, studying the new-humans. 'The undead.'

'Look,' said Loca, pointing to an area in the projection as Ghost Team Five arrived close to her. The rasping of their exoskeleton's metal boots on the fragmented ground made more noise than anyone would have wanted.

Both teams stared at the scene of hundreds of neo-humans battling each other in a frenzied state. They lunged and hacked one another with a lack of thought; pure animalistic ferocity, reminiscent of a hyena pack over a new kill.

'I place the Identifier...' Loca paused, assessing. 'Fourteen klicks, in the direction of this trash heap of a planet's north. Through those hordes ahead of us.'

'Yo, something just happened,' Nightflare said, he was a trooper of Ghost Team Five, who had crouched close by. He searched to make sense of his GCD's readings. 'We just lost one of our canine units. Could just be a communication issue with its receiver.'

'Get a visual,' Nightflare's commanding officer ordered, from the left of him.

'Don't bother,' Black Knight said. 'We've been discovered.' He raised his weapon and turned to his right. 'Set all the canines to defensive mode. Right now.'

No one saw what he took aim at, but they soon heard a roar muted by the howl of the dust wind. Then came a wave of multiple roars. The animalistic screams dispersed through the mist, becoming all-surrounding. MKEPX13's butts clanged against exoskeleton metal as they readied to fire everything they had.

'They're coming,' Nightflare said in a rush of breath. His face had turned red.

'Ghost Teams,' Tombstone said. 'Watch out for crossfire. Stay out of the canines' line of sight.'

Roars and the sound of bodies crashing onto the crumbled

surface got louder. Black bodies of neo-humans appeared through the mist. Four of them felt the sting of soul redeemers housed on the backs of canine drones and shattered. The three that made it through were intercepted by the prejudice of Ghost Team gunfire. Tombstone commanded Loca to inform the Ring of the situation, yelling at her to make haste.

'Multiple hostiles are converging on our location,' Loca said on the comms link over weapons fire. 'From the north and eighty degrees east.'

'Acknowledged,' Colonel Marcs voice on their radio. 'I need all teams to fan out and keep advancing to the target LZ. This is what you trained for.'

The Black Knight watched as The Boogieman used his soul redeemer to rip apart the body of the last neo-human that charged them. As its body disintegrated, a blue mist of energy drifted in the air.

With a ceasing of the firefight, the soldiers reflected on the unusual behavior of the attackers.

'That was a lot easier than usual,' Tombstone said.

'Must be the atmosphere,' Peacemaker said. 'It's fucking with them.'

'It's the gravity,' Black Knight said. 'They were stronger in Earth's weaker gravity.'

'You guys seeing that glowing shit over there?' said Wingman as he watched the blue mist-like energy, there were at least eight of them. 'They appeared straight after we killed the monster-men.' They began to converge into more of a spherical form and attracted tiny pieces of the planet's black rock up towards it.

'Shit!' Loca said. She noticed how the floating rock fragments appeared to clump together and fuse around the hovering energy source.

'We need to move,' Black Knight said, with his keen senses. 'The creatures are reforming.'

'Shit!' Wingman said, the sight made sweat trickle down his face.

'Holy shit!' Tombstone said before yelling Loca's name. 'Plot waypoints for the safest path towards the Identifier. Right now!' He then shouted at the other Ghost Team to get moving. They kept themselves spaced out enough that each team were within visual range on the broken terrain.

Loca began panting as she analyzed the horror on her screen. 'More hostiles advancing on us from all directions. Getting to the target without being detected is going to be hard.'

'About as hard as your momma's dick, Loca,' Peacemaker said as he marched forward. 'Just keep your eyes on those damn scanners. I don't want one of those things putting their paws up my ass.'

The repetitive sound of weapons-fire broke through the screaming wind.

'Came from behind us,' said the Boogieman's deep voice, swinging his heavy soul redeemer around.

Shortly after the gunfire came the screams on the shared radio. Wingman saw the gunfire light up the purple sky.

'GT Nine is under fire,' Wingman said, he tried his best to block out the ambient noise to listen in on the radio chatter.

'Haul ass!' ordered Tombstone. 'Let's get the fuck out of here before they surround us.'

CHAPTER TEN

TO ACT,
ONE MUST
BE INSANE

All the screaming and gunfire had stopped.

Joshua kept as far away from the room's door as he could. He knew someone waited outside, and the silence petrified him more than the screams. With a thunderous bang, a force struck the metal door, and it indented with a bulge that covered the length and width of the door itself. He felt that he was a stone's throw away from fainting. A second bang and the door ripped off the hinges; its heavy weight clanged on the metallic floor.

He stood in shock at the sight of a neo-human standing in the doorway, its large, grotesque form incapable of getting through the opening without either careful maneuvering or destroying the doorway. Its neck hunched low, with one side crafted shorter than the other, making it look like a failed attempted at a hellish genetic experimentation.

'As you have freed my soul from madness, I have freed yours, Joshua Smith,' the neo-human said. No sound projected through the air; Joshua heard the words from inside his head. The telepathic means by which the neo-humans communicated extended to humans as well.

'Jeremiah,' Joshua uttered. He ventured out the doorway toward the eight-foot giant, stepping over the fallen door. Venturing closer he saw the RM-V9 series mangled on the floor, its quantum processors still moving the motors of its limbs. 'I thank you.'

'Another is more deserved of your thanks.'

'Another? Who?'

'The one who had turned on the artificial gravity and unlocked my prison doors. They left me a message on the walls, inscribed in blood. The message was two words "Help Smith".'

Joshua was confused, though Hannerman showed enough care and goodness to assist him, the old man was not the murdering type. Perhaps Hannerman was working with someone. Despite knowledge that Black Knight was an enemy of the Circle, he seemed to hate Joshua just as intensely. Joshua wasted no time on the mystery as he grabbed his tattered jacket which he hadn't worn in some time and its LEDs flashed as he flung it on.

'I need you to help me get to the Quantum Room.'

'Yes master.' The inhuman skull of Jeremiah, with its sharp horns, turned as he stepped to leave.

'Wait. I'm not your master, Jeremiah Nwakande. I'm asking this as a friend, as a brother. One man to another. Will you help me, please?'

Jeremiah paused; his five red eyes focused on the man. The horns on his ginormous head fluctuating seemingly by their own consciousness. 'Help me to feel the warmth of the African sun once more, and I will aid you.'

'Ok.'

***

The loud security alarm throbbed furiously in Joshua's eardrum and ruined any chance of them reaching the Quantum Room undetected. They periodically heard Colonel Marcs and his executive officer's voice on the facility's speakers ordering them to cease and give themselves up or be killed. But Joshua's blood flowed with the force of an avalanche through his veins. A security personnel spotted them, true to their orders, they opened fire immediately. More converged on them. Defenseless, he shielded himself behind his neo-human accomplice from the weapons-fire as Jeremiah tore through them.

A devilish symphony of sounds bombarded Joshua's ears; screams and the cracking of bones as Jeremiah punched and pulled torsos apart. But he soon heard groans of agony emanating from his inhuman accomplice. Though stripped of the full extent of human senses, the rifle rounds, kinetic energy penetration projectiles and the brief surges of magnetic Higgs boson frequency disruptor fire broke sections of his exoskeleton and inflicted grievous pain. Joshua temporarily lost his hearing due to the deafening impact of the shells against Jeremiah's body.

His traumatized ears still ringing, and Jeremiah down on his spikey, oversized knees, Joshua looked up and saw Moreau and five armed men. They were accompanied by two robot guards holding Ghost Team MKEPX13's rifles; it was confirmation to Joshua he was trapped in a living nightmare. Behind them, the entrance to the Quantum Room. There was a pause in the firing upon Moreau's command, and with it, the hallway stopped vibrating.

'Smith!' shouted Moreau from afar. 'Stop where you are and hand yourselves in peacefully. Or else you will regret this day. I will imprison and torment your souls for eternity. Before long, you both will beg for mortality. This is your final warning.'

Joshua could hear the distorted vocal sounds from Jeremiah's vertical head-opening that passed for his mouth and sensed the neo-human's pain. One sustained blast from a soul redeemer that the Circle's men held would revert Jeremiah back to Olympus and the young physicist would be alone.

'Jeremiah,' Joshua whispered. 'Don't be afraid of what you are. You are not an abomination, but an angel. If God exists, his strength flows through you and with it, you can do his wonders. The ones to blame for our fates now stand in our path. Rise up, we can conquer them.'

Jeremiah raised his head towards the men and opened his jagged mouth, releasing a terrifying roar. He leapt an inhuman distance and crashed onto the security forces who fired upon him.

With the neo-human distracted, Moreau seized his moment. Caught defenseless, Joshua watched Moreau remove a handgun from his liquid-filled jumpsuit and point it at him.

'In another life, Joshua, we could have been… better. But the Circle's will must be done. So long.'

There were two bangs, muffled by the background gunfire. To Moreau's surprise, the shots to Joshua's chest didn't drop him. Though unconvinced he could have missed, Moreau fired again. The young physicist remained on his feet, unscathed. Moreau looked to the floor and noticed a light. His eyes finally distinguished that the light came for an electronic device—it was a

GCD. He yelped, knowing he had been outwitted.

The pale-faced man turned to his side, and Joshua greeted him with a punch to his sweaty cheek, quickly followed by a forceful kick to his ribs.

'*Motherfucker!*' the real-life Joshua yelled as his augmented reality decoy disappeared.

Moreau fell, belly to the floor. Joshua looked around to make sure they were clear of immediate danger. Jeremiah's neo-human strength made a horrific scene of the Circle's agents, only the R-MEN remained. Though missing limbs from Jeremiah's onslaught, they tussled relentlessly.

Joshua noticed a liquid by his foot, it had pooled around Moreau's sprawled out body. Moreau reanimated with a painful gasp of air and turned over onto his back, revealing the source of the blue liquid. Joshua's kick must have punctured his suit; there was an obvious whole in the abdominal section, and it deflated as a result.

Moreau raised his gun at him with last ditched strength, but Joshua grabbed his sweaty hands before he could fire. 'Do you know why the caged puma roared?' he asked Joshua, wincing from each desperate breath. 'The…caged…bur-bur-bird ssssings.' The old man then released painful screams before he finally stopped breathing, and his body went limp.

In a cautious manner, Joshua pulled the gun out from his grasp.

After a hard-fought victory against the R-MEN, Jeremiah escorted Joshua along the corridors until they made it to the entrance of the Quantum Room. But the threat of the Circle still loomed. Colonel Marcs would no doubt be in the Control Room, gathering his forces and strategizing effective ways to kill him. Security personnel from throughout the vast Ring would be converging upon them. They were effectively boxed in. As the chatter on radios of the slain men intensified, he knew the two of them wouldn't stand a chance.

Jeremiah agreed to hold off their pursuers while Joshua entered the Quantum Room, breathless with adrenalin pumping through him. Most of the room's personnel had fled long before they arrived on reports that they were heading for the Transcender. Hannerman, however, was still present. The old man stood dead still on sight of Joshua holding a gun. His wrinkle face turned whiter and eyes widened.

'Joshua look out!' Hannerman shouted.

Two gunshots followed Hannerman's cries that narrowly missed Joshua. Luckily for him, his attacker was a poor shot.

A familiar voice shouted out ancient Greek. His fear shifting him into a hyper-alert state. Self-preservation was the first law of nature and the only thing on his mind. He whipped around and saw someone holding a handgun. In fractions of a second, quicker than he could identify his attacker, he fired back one shot. It was the first time he had held a gun before; the first time he had killed anyone. Not just anyone, Dr. Zahurska was his victim.

Hannerman approached and took the weapon from him, noticing how unresponsive Joshua became as he watched Zahurska's lifeless body on the floor. The betrayal of someone who had befriended him, his act of killing; the shock had overwhelmed him.

'It's alright, Joshua. There was nothing else you could do.'

It took a while to overcome his shock, but his adrenaline eventually kicked him back to reality.

'Thanks for helping me escape,' Joshua said. 'I need to get to Olympus right now.'

'I must be honest. I never played a part in your release, Joshua.'

The young scientist was bewildered.

'But I'm glad you're here,' Hannerman said, giving his token smile. 'I want to help. Cassius was right, all men at some time are masters of their fate. But look, Joshua, I must let you know, Homerton Hospital suffered a complete blackout. Sav—'

'I know. I'm going anyway.'

'Why?'

The physicist rushed towards an exoskeleton suit, which hung on a harness, and jumped into it, spinning his body around so his back slammed against it first. Robotic arms quickly began to connect the exoskeleton to his back and on his limbs. 'I saw an Unknown, a little girl, her parents at her bedside. I thought of all those souls who don't have anyone to fight for them, whose loved ones are sitting in Hives at their bedside every day, praying that someone who *can* help them *will* help them. I've got to try.'

'The situation is a disaster, Joshua, most of the Ghost Teams have been slaughtered, our mission has been a failure thus far.'

'I don't care, I've got to go.' Below his right wrist, a metal armband coiled and snapped as it locked. A display and status lights powered on, and the suit came to life in a myriad of lights and mechanical noise. Joshua stepped off the harness feeling a sense of weightlessness, the exosuit was now doing the heavy lifting.

'Listen to me, there are millions of indestructible creatures that are going to kill you before you get anywhere near the Identifier. You don't stand a chance, so let's find another way. Life is too precious my friend, don't throw it away, even for a worthy cause. In spite of Savannah, despite of your pain, your life matters, Joshua. It always will.'

Joshua glanced at the old man eyes and saw something, something he had seen only when Hannerman spoke of his wife. An onrush of emotion came over him. He placed a hand on Hannerman's frail shoulder. 'Thank you, Frank. For opening my eyes to so much that I never saw.'

'You cannot let your tragedy define who you are.'

'I can, if I use it to become more… than who I was.'

'Look, perhaps, in time we could—'

'It's now or never, Frank. I know it sounds ridiculous and the odds are stacked completely against me. There's no logic, rationale, or science that can explain what I feel, but there are moments in life where you just have to walk with fai... that you just have to believe. Show me the way to the Identifier, we can do this… we shall… *we must.*'

Hannerman shook his head with a lack of certainty in his reply then nodded. 'Alright, then we don't have much time.' He commanded the computer's AR interface to activate and then his wrinkly hands worked feverishly as he inputted commands on the aform terminal. 'I'm modifying the corrective code now which will free the minds without making them slaves. The Identifier is located within Olympus's great monument. Once inside the structure, head for the nerve center of the Identifier. You will find a wall containing seven orbs. The orbs are laid out in the pattern of—'

'A circle?'

Hannerman smiled. 'We're not the most original up here. Place the mind code in the center of the circle.'

'I don't know how to thank you, Frank.'

'Live to become old and stupid like me. That will be thanks enough. Now you've got three enemies; the neo-human hordes on the planet, and what's left of the Ghost Teams who are going to try and stop you if they discover what you're up to. The third enemy is—'

'Is time. If the Ghost Teams insert their control code before me, it will be too late. Piece of cake, huh!'

Hannerman handed Joshua the same circular glass and metallic capsule used to free Jeremiah's mind, and also given to Ghost Team One to insert into Olympus's Identifier.

'Oh, don't damage the suit's armband. It's a mini power generator made from ultrafaron-steel alloy that stops the exoskeleton's rear power banks running low.'

'You've strapped a mini bomb to my arm?'

'And wait, I have to give you the injections.' Hannerman quickly reached for a syringe, which had a lengthy needle at its end. 'This is going to hurt.' Joshua winced and tensed up as Hannerman injected him in his deltoid through a gap in the exoskeleton's armor. Afterwards, he lifted the suit's metal chest plating and jabbed the psyched-up younger man with the needle in his heart. Finally, he injected him in his spine. Joshua's puffing quickly subdued, and he looked at Hannerman strangely for a few seconds.

'That's it? I barely felt a thing.'

Hannerman raised an eyebrow. 'Just wait.'

Joshua stepped onto the Transcender's platform and the machine got louder as its energy cells powered up. 'A trillionth of a second to cross trillions of miles.'

'I don't have time to quantumize a weapon for you,' Hannerman said, shouting over the noise of the energy build up, 'you'll be going in only holding your…code, in your hand.'

'I guess it's better than the alternative.'

'Joshua…' Hannerman hesitated, struggling to convey his words seeing the young man's determination. 'This is insane.'

Joshua remained silent for a moment, contemplating somberly what he was about to do. 'In order to act, one must be somewhat insane. Because a reasonably sensible man is satisfied with only… thinking.'

Hannerman exhaled. 'I'll guide you as much as I can from here.'

CHAPTER ELEVEN

WHAT IS HIS NAME

Everything turned to a bright white light. His sensory organs were awash in a bath of all extremes, all at the same moment. The flood of whiteness vanished instantaneously yet Joshua's rematerialized body could not take in his new surroundings, despite how badly he wanted to. His legs were rubbery, his stomach churned; it was like the worst bout of travel sickness he'd ever had. With the exoskeleton lining his arms, he forcefully grabbed his breast plating, feeling as if his chest was close to exploding. Despite the cocktail of drugs and his supportive armor, the power of four times Earth's gravity was crushing him down.

'Joshua are you there?' said Hannerman's voice. It came from the exoskeleton's headguard.

Joshua fell to the hard, black surface with an intense groan. He squeezed the ultrafaron rock, gritting his teeth. His lungs felt on fire when he opened his mouth to reply. 'This must be what purgatory feels like.'

'Shake it off, young man.'

'Easy for you to say.' The kick of the drugs wore off, and he finally gathered the strength to rise to his feet. His determined eyes peered out toward the slanted pyramids and focused on the Circle's giant monument in the purple Olympian skyline. The great wings of the structure, obscured by patches of grayish-purple clouds, towered in the distance like they belonged to a giant eagle. 'Incredible!'

'I've dropped you in at a closer proximity to the Identifier than we did the Ghost Teams. You're about eleven kilometers away from the Identifier. Hopefully, the Ghost Teams would have created a diversion, giving you a clear path.'

'Hopefully.' Joshua glanced around at the rubble of black, broken stone and the remnants of diagonal pyramids that pierced through the misty sky. He had never seen a landscape that compared to what his eyes beheld. 'By God!' He noticed a sound similar to the zapping of high voltage electricity. Glancing behind him, Joshua saw a white, spherical disruption; a giant orb. Its rim rippled with the energy that had torn through the space-time fabric.

'You'll see the focal point behind you,' Hannerman said. 'You'll need to get back to it as quickly as you can. Or you'll be trapped on Olympus.'

He could accept death. But the thought of being marooned on the other side of the universe, with no possible means of returning to Earth, made his body shake. 'I can do this.'

'Head to the great monument ahead. The Identifier is inside.'

He took off in what he intended to be a slow jog, but the unexpected speed of his acceleration made him tumble over. The exoskeleton's electronic and pneumatic systems had gifted him with unexpected power.

Despite Hannerman telling him to slow his momentum to avoid being detected, Joshua dashed towards his destination with a sprint, hoping to insert the mind-code as fast as he could. The exoskeleton made it feel almost effortless, helping him to leap over huge debris. He noticed a few white, spherical objects scattered around the city that varied in diameter.

'What are those giant, white spheres?'

'Those were the neo-human's transportation system. Most have been damaged in their berserk state. Only the neo-humans can operate them.'

Joshua's thoughts were that the small spheres must have functioned like cars while the large ones were the buses or trains. Another sight forced him to stop in his tracks. On the ground laid a corpse, human; the clothes and tactical gear drenched in blood. The head was nowhere to be seen, and the arms and exoskeleton mangled.

'Frank, I just discovered a dead Ghost Team operator.'

'I've not had any reports from the Ghost Teams since I locked Marcs out the system. It's best you avoid them. Is there a weapon?'

'I can't find it. I'll keep moving.'

'Hurry Joshua,' Hannerman said.

Joshua sensed an unusual distress in his voice.

'What's wrong, Frank?'

'Jeremiah... I think they got him. His soul has been reverted. I've locked down the Quantum Room, but Marcs is resourceful, I won't be able to keep him out for long.'

Joshua tried to shrug off the dire news. Jeremiah's mind would be corrupted by the Identifier once he was ripped back through space and reformed a new body on Olympus.

'Joshua, if you manage to free the souls, you'll be freeing the souls of the Circle's neo-human agents as well—they'll come after you. You'll also free Savannah's neo-human consciousness, she will still exist there.'

'I know. I don't know what I would do if I saw her.'

'Well if you hang around long enough you will see her. Before the hospital lost power, I had been monitoring her brain scans and I created a mind map for her. I was trying to help you save her. Within the corrective code is a message that will be sent to her mind telling her to locate you at the Identifier.'

Joshua soon began to hear uncomfortably familiar growls. Turning around, he laid eyes on four neo-humans, shoulders hunched, arms hanging at their side. Their vertical mouths gaped opened when they saw him. He took off, and they gave chase. As he had anticipated, their speed was no match for him in his exoskeleton, which had also gifted him with the ability to take huge bounds over the broken artificial structures. His problem was that his pursuers were relentless, and also, they attracted more of their kind. He watched as they poured in from numerous angles, stomping the ground, roaring in murderous fury. He knew that it was only a matter of time before he would be cut off on all sides.

'I'm in trouble, Frank,' he said, gasping for air.

'Think of something, quickly.'

'I'm not going to make it. They're coming in fast.'

'You're going to have to find somewhere to hide. Quick Joshua!'

Ahead of him, he spotted a cliff edge and sprinted towards it with desperate breaths. Out of options, he leaped off the precipice, falling onto a pile of rubble, which once formed part of an Olympian megastructure. As he crashed down, the loose fragments of ultrafaron material gave way, and he sank into the ruin. Submerged in the wreckage, Joshua felt the pain of multiple cuts and scrapes along the sections of his skin that weren't covered by titanium alloy. It was too dark to see anything, but he heard a crashing thud, followed by many more. There was a constant rasping as dozens of footsteps darted upon the fragmented rocky soil. Through gaps in the debris that secluded him, Joshua saw the neo-humans combing the dense rubble trying to find him, toppling over and fighting each other. Trying to calm his breathing, he saw more creatures arriving, then more. Two fought over the corpse of a Ghost Team operator; the body continually ripped into multiple pieces.

As his stomach began to churn, he came to the harsh realization that his bravery was over-cavalier. He wouldn't be able to make it to the Identifier, at least not alone, and defenseless. The pursuers hacked away at the rubble, closing in on him from every angle. Their demented wills spurred them to hunt him until they claimed his soul, or he was dead. They had smashed through so much of his hiding place that he felt they could now see him through the gaps in the ruins.

As his hope faded, he thought he could hear a sound over the nearby growls of his fiendish pursuers. The neo-humans detected it too. They turned to face the direction of its origin and without much thought, they took off toward it.

'Frank, I think there's someone still out here,' Joshua said, after the neo-humans distanced themselves from him and he regained his ability to breathe. 'One of the Ghost Team soldiers is still alive.'

'I'm not aware of any communication from anyone. Are you sure?'

'I'm hearing something, I think it's gunfire. I'm going to head towards it.'

'That is ill-advised Joshua, the Ghost Team operators may not be friendly.'

'Perhaps, but remaining here is certain death. And one of the Ghost Team soldiers might be on our side.'

'Try to—' A painful yelp stopped Hannerman midsentence.

Joshua was certain he heard the muffled echo of a blunt mass dropping on the floor.

'Frank? Frank, talk to me? What's going on?'

A voice broke through the low-level radio static. 'The not so good doctor will no longer be able to help you anymore.'

He knew instantly who it was, but his mind refused to accept it. 'Zahurska?' the young man uttered; his pitch elevated. 'You're… alive?'

'You should have killed me when you had the chance.'

'Why… why are you doing this—'

'If a drug dealer or pimp had given you a hundred thousand surons to complete your experiments, would you have taken it? Even if it meant being indebted to them? It doesn't matter what you think the Circle is, this world is ice cold, Joshua, and a girl's got to eat. You think I'm going to go back to sleeping on sewerage flooded streets for some sense of morality?'

He quickly got over his shock—thanks to the anger coursing through him. 'No, I wouldn't take it—and those flooded streets aren't as cold as life without a soul. What have you done to Frank? If you've harmed him, I swear I'll do even worse when I find you.'

'I don't think so,' another voiced replied.

The man's words conveyed power and a confidence that stunned him more than Zahurska' incredible resurrection.

'You thought Moreau was your biggest threat? He's nothing compared to me. I've been fighting all my life, son. Colonel Anderson T. Marcs is not going to lose a fight now. You want to go to war with the Circle of Hermes? You have no idea who you're fucking with, son. You trying to save your lil' lady, huh? We are going to find both her human and neo-human bodies and we're going to lock them away so deep into the pits of Tartarus you will never find her.'

'No!'

'Yes!' Marcs' word lingered with a chill. 'That's just the start of it. And your old man? Oh, he's going to be backstroking through the shit. I'm going to crucify him upside down—you can believe *that. We... are... power.* Now cease and desist, son, and get your narrow ass back to the focal point ASAP. Or we will make you suffer—'

Joshua had heard enough, and he ripped his radio off of his head guard. His lungs near-bursting from the deepest of breaths, he battled through his fears, knowing that if he crumbled now, all would be lost forever. He took a peek out the gap and saw that the neo-humans had dispersed after hearing the gunshots. But they didn't venture far, and there was enough of them to eventually swarm him if he was seen and couldn't find somewhere to hide again. But he seized his chance.

Joshua leapt through his cover and made a dash for it. His would-be killers roared at him before giving chase. In his peripheral vision, he caught sight of creatures gaining on him from both sides. Fear stumbled him and he toppled. Looking around, he saw a neo-human launching at him from close range. His arms rose in front of his face in hopes that the metal running along his forearm bones would shield him from a deathblow. Rifle rounds broke apart the creature's midsection, reducing it to a pile of fragments.

Joshua turned towards the trajectory of the bullets and saw Sergeant Tombstone on one knee, squeezing hard on the trigger. He was drenched in a mixture of sweat and blood, and his exoskeleton's right arm harness was mangled. Three more attackers pounced at Joshua and he pushed his body backwards in an attempt to avoid them. The intense energy beam of a soul redeemer ripped apart Joshua's attackers. In his close proximity, the heat and light of the energy forced him to shield his eyes. He could hear the carnage of gunfire from multiple sources, but he struggled to open his eyes again; it was too painful. He had developed arc eye, as though his naked eye had been exposed to a welder's torch.

Joshua heard Tombstone shouting "watch out" and "cover the rear" but all he could do was curl up in a ball and pray, feeling the impact vibrations on the broken landscape.

The carnage eventually calmed.

'Get up!' said an unmistakably deep voice.

Joshua painfully forced his eyes open. Towering above him stood The Boogieman. The giant never looked at the young man, only panning his heavy soul redeemer searching for more hostiles—with a face that told its own stories of the horrors it had witnessed. Behind him, Loca hustled to help Wingman to his feet. He appeared to be struggling with injuries; four claw marks on his torso suggested that a blow had broken through his exoskeleton and had also ripped through his black combat uniform and his flesh.

He saw Peacemaker stoop low, removing the ammunition from Nightflare whose body lay contorted on the sloping terrain as though his legs were broken. The gravely injured man's hand reached out to Peacemaker and the Ghost Team One operator used his boot to push the bloodied hand back. He shot the man in the chest saying "sayonara" for parting words.

Surveying the surroundings, Joshua saw that the neo-humans had disappeared, and numerous auras of energy drifted in the sky.

'We're getting tired of saving your ass,' Peacemaker said, making exhausted steps towards Joshua.

Joshua glanced behind the man and saw more dead soldiers.

'Where's Black Knight?' he asked them.

'He's inside some monster-man's guts by now,' Peacemaker said.

'MIA,' Tombstone said. 'We were ambushed. Everyone's dead.'

'He might be still out there, sir,' said Loca. 'I'll keep running a sensor sweep. So far, he's—'

'I said he's dead,' Peacemaker said, baring his browning teeth.

'Wingman, Boogieman—monitor our perimeter,' ordered Tombstone. He turned back to Joshua. 'What are you doing here, civilian? I thought I told you to stay on the Ring?'

Joshua had now noticed how both men drew nearer to him cautiously.

'I... I needed...'

'Where is the code, homeboy?' Peacemaker said. He watched how Joshua's startled body stepped backwards and he unleashed a deranged smile. 'That's right, the colonel apprehended that old fart and informed us about your bullshit crusade.'

'Wait, Tombstone,' Joshua said, addressing the commanding officer, knowing it was pointless pleading to a madman. 'The Circle is evil. They lied to you. They are trying to rule over the neo-humans by brainwashing them and turning Olympus into a world of slaves. This is how the souls of the neo-humans got corrupted. The code I have will heal them. I'm telling you the truth. Help me guys.'

As soon as Joshua stopped speaking, Tombstone pointed his weapon at him.

'That's a righteous cause you're fighting for, Dr. Smith. But you're not seeing the far bigger picture. We intend to destroy the Earth. Only Olympus will exist, and we will rule over it like the Greek Gods we descended from. This completes the circle. So, I'm going to need you to give me that capsule.'

'We need to get moving, man,' Wingman said in a panicked outburst. 'They're coming. Range – four hundred meters and closing.'

'It's cool,' Peacemaker said. 'We've just found ourselves here a decoy.' His mouth hung open like he was about to growl. 'Fresh bait! We already knew all that shit you fucking nerd. They've already guaranteed us a seat at the table.' Peacemaker pulled out his cutlass, and to Joshua's horror, he continued advancing. Coolant lubricant leaked from his exoskeleton's right knee-jolt and every time Peacemaker lifted his leg Joshua could see the surge of strain that flashed across his face, but he smiled, relishing each second.

Loca watched on, seemingly caught up in the situation,

conflicted by her feelings on what was about to happen, despite all the Circle had promised her. Wingman and The Boogieman remained focused on neutralizing the neo-humans closing in on them.

'Hand over the capsule, Smith,' Tombstone said. 'That's an order.'

'You heard the boss, bitch,' Peacemaker said. 'Give it here.'

'Wait!' Loca said, trying to stop Peacemaker. Not fully confident in her reasons why. 'Let's just—'

'Shut up!' said the maniac. He snarled and turned back to Joshua. 'Better yet, I think I'll make you swallow it and then I'll gut it out of you.'

'Please, don't,' Joshua said, wishing he had the means to defend himself. He wanted to run but he remembered when Peacemaker had flung his cutlass into the terrorist with authority and precision. A knife in the back was not how he wanted to die. Joshua raised both his palms out toward the men and prayed for mercy.

Peacemaker laughed again. 'You know that's the same thing my momma said right before I slit her throat... from ear to ear.'

As he raised his hand to strike Joshua, something hit Peacemaker's exposed neck and dropped him, severing his head. Tombstone whipped his rifle around to a Ghost Team operator covered in blood from head to toe. He paused for merely a split-second; enough time for him to conclude his assessment. He fired at Black Knight and the African soldier took cover before returning fire. Loca quickly made up her mind and fired at Tombstone. Under their heavy onslaught, he retreated and disappeared amongst the wrecked structures.

Wingman and The Boogieman hadn't noticed the unfolding skirmish, as berserk neo-humans pounced at them. Two neo-humans grabbed Wingman. Black Knight's rifle rounds defragmented one of his comrade's attacker but the other, with its mammoth size and strength, ripped Wingman's upper torso apart from his legs as he screamed. Before Black Knight could destroy the other attacker, his teammate lay dead.

The Boogieman's soul redeemer inflicted the most damage, and it annihilated the remaining hostiles.

'Clear!' the giant man said. He was drenched in sweat. Despite the aid of the exoskeleton's motors and pneumatics, the intensity of battle made him rest the soul redeemer on the ground to recover his energy.

'Not for long,' Black Knight said.

Joshua followed Black Knight's eyes to the floating vapors of energy and saw how they had begun to attract the rocky, ultrafaron earth below. He gasped, knowing instantly what it meant.

'I knew you wouldn't be dead,' Loca said to Black Knight. 'So, what the hell do we do now?' asked Loca. 'Tombstone has the capsule with the code. Are we staying on mission?'

'You must get to the Identifier and insert my mind code,' Joshua said.

'Really?' said Loca, 'Look around—we're not in motherfucking Kansas anymore, pendejo.'

'Please hear me,' Joshua said, stepping in front of them. 'This is wrong—all of this. Forget about everything that's happened in the past, history is going to be decided by the choice you make right here, right now. And history will either condemn us or hopefully absolve us. We all might have done unforgivable wrong in our lives,' Joshua's eyes locked onto Black Knight for that moment. 'Here's our chance to make things right. To save so many lost souls.'

'Why did you come,' Black Knight said, 'if you thought you couldn't save her?'

'I didn't come here for her. I came for all of them. Every life is just as important as Savannah's.'

'Look amigo, everyone else is dead,' Loca said. Sweat-logged strands of her hair stuck to her caramel skin. 'There are too many of them.'

Joshua shook his head. 'Man was imbued with the potential to overcome impossible odds. We *must* try; maybe that's the essence of why we exist in the first place, to do as much good in our physical form as we can. Because that's the only life worth living. Together we can… we shall… *we must.*'

'We will!' Black Knight said, walking up to the physicist. There was a clink as he stepped on Peacemaker's cutlass. 'The souls of man deserve to be judged by God alone and none will escape his judgement. I'll stand by your side, Smith. And while I stand, no weapon that is formed against thee shall prosper. This is the heritage of the servants of the Lord, and their righteousness is of me, saith the Lord.'

Loca and The Boogieman only stared at their comrade. No

doubt surprised by his religious revelations. Loca kept her eyebrows raised and her lips pressed thinly together in anger; her red eyes glaring into the Black Knight's eyes. 'So, you were the enemy all this time? The Builders of Jericho? And you've been playing us the whole fucking time.'

'Yes, but I never played you, L' Black Knight said. 'We don't have much time. Are you with us?'

'You're the highest in the chain of command, Corporal,' Loca said. 'Whatever you say I'm with you... always!'

Black Knight gave a thankful nod of his head before turning to The Boogieman who had remained customarily silent and with his trademark mean mug.

'Ermm...' said Joshua, 'What about you, Mr. Boogieman?'

The muscle-bound soldier refused to respond. Instead, he lifted his soul redeemer and came toward Joshua and Black Knight. Joshua could make out a high-pitched noise as the weapon built up its charge. Neo-human claws had given him four nasty slashes that sliced through his chest plating, and he bled badly from the wounds. But you would've had to inform him of it for him to be aware. Joshua cautiously backed away, sensing the worst, as his weapon could take out all of them, and if not, the giant's bare hands could still do the job. The goliath stopped and faced Black Knight, his dark visor concealing his eyes. His massive muscles rippled and contracted.

'Did you have to ask?' he said to Black Knight.

'I didn't,' Black Knight said with composure, 'he did.' Pointing at the physicist. 'I already know what your answer is.' At six foot two inches, Black Knight still had to look high up to stare him dead in his visor.

The Boogieman stood silent, increasing the anxiety of the group. Loca's finger lingered on her trigger fearing what would happen if the big man refused.

'I'm with you, Black,' said The Boogieman.

***

They journeyed through the treacherous alien city, while the crazed neo-humans hunted them. Black Knight kept asking Loca to perform sensor sweeps for signs of their former Sergeant. He seemed to be more concerned about Tombstone than the

Olympian hordes and with good reason. He knew the Polish soldier well, he was one of Marcs best and most skilled soldiers; an expert in the art of killing. He had detected long ago that Tombstone's uncharismatic persona was merely a mask, and underneath was the face of pure evil.

The great monument of the Circle seemed to stretch over their heads, so grand was its height. But they were still some kilometers away. An all-out battle was what they had dreaded, and the ammunition the Ghost Team operators carried in their backpacks quickly dwindled against the waves of onslaught.

Joshua gazed into the distance behind them and saw a neo-human complete its reconstitution of the energy mist. The native horde kept growing in number; there would be no way they could have gone back the way they came. But through the carnage Joshua had found a lifeline. 'Over there, look,' he shouted. He ran toward a metal object covered by large chunks of rock, while The Boogieman and Black Knight's firepower kept the onrushes off his heels. Loca followed him. 'It's one of your drones.' Joshua looked up at the sloping pyramid above his head. 'Part of the structure collapsed and fell on it.'

'Ayúdame!' Loca said. 'Give me a hand.' She grabbed the hefty piece of pyramid fragment, using the ancient Egyptian style indentations to get a firm grip. Together, mustering their full strength, they lifted the material enough for the robotic dog to pry itself free, using its front legs while its back limbs dragged.

'Both its hind legs are damaged,' Joshua said. He couldn't help feeling compassion for the robot, while watching it trying to stabilize itself. But most importantly, strapped on its back rested the extra firepower they needed.

'Canine unit,' Loca called out over the noise of Black Knight's weapons-fire. 'Is your soul redeemer operational?'

'Affirmative,' replied the distorted computerized voice.

Joshua quickly removed the damaged casing of its left rear leg to access the electronics. 'This leg's beyond repair, but its controller is still intact. I can use it and a few of its undamaged joint drives on the right leg.'

'Just do it fast,' she replied, under pressure as she defended them from approaching neo-humans by firing her MKEPX13 rifle. 'This place is fucking crawling.' A neo-human launched itself at her, knocking her to the ground and the rifle away from her grasp.

The inhuman went in for the kill, raising its sixteen claws to claim her. Her fight or flight moment had come, and she chose to not go peacefully. Screaming with rage, she grabbed her tech-baton from her side and swung it with all her strength. It clanged against her attacker's oversized hand, shattering it. The creature howled like it could feel the sensation of pain. Loca saw the blue energy seeping from its missing hand, dispersing like smoke shifting its form in the wind. The blood pouring from her nose increased her adrenalin. Wildly, she hacked away at the abdomen of the eight-foot monster.

A sudden blast of energy flung her backwards. The force of a soul redeemer's beam destroyed the creature and flash burned her face, like the pain of hours of exposure in the hottest of suns.

'You ok?' Joshua asked, worried about how she toppled. The canine unit limped on three legs, thanks to his expertise, with its weapon glowing.

'Do I look fucking ok?' Loca yelled at Joshua. She rose back to her feet.

'Loca,' Black Knight said. He and the big man ran to her side. 'Any sign of Tombstone?'

The drone's soul redeemer was a massive help in their desperate moment. It awarded the resilient woman the breathing space to shrug off the sting of the burns. She stooped low to analyze her GCD. 'He's disabled his tracking ID. Motion sensors still aren't able to distinguish between him and the hostiles.'

'The Sarge is one mean son of a bitch,' The Boogieman said. 'He's still out there.'

'For real,' Loca said. 'I heard that shit about him killing his family.'

'No,' Joshua said, puzzled. 'That's not what he said to me.'

'It *was* what he said to you,' Black Knight replied. 'The Circle discovered his wife and son were Jews. They offered him a choice to prove his loyalty.'

'He said they were killed by a monster,' Joshua uttered, remembering the Sergeant's story, the horrific truth shocked him like a lightning bolt. 'Dear God! What kind of…we need to get to the Identifier quickly,' Joshua said. Their neo-human pursuers became second place in his concerns for the first time since arriving on Olympus. 'Before he's able to insert his corrective code.'

Loca and Black Knight shared a glance at each other.

'He doesn't know?' Loca said.

Joshua's head bounced between the two of them. 'Know what?'

'The capsule we were given,' Black Knight said, 'the one Tombstone still holds; it does not contain a code which will cure their minds. It contains technology which will allow the Circle of Hermes to control the Identifier—remotely.'

'I guess,' Loca said, 'they wanted to be able to control it from Earth.'

'No.' Joshua uttered in deep thought. 'It's not just that. The process of transcending souls was costly and inefficient. The neo-humans abducting the souls, however, isn't. They're going to continue allowing neo-humans to breach Earth and abduct as many souls as possible and let the Earth be destroyed.'

They sprinted to the base of the great monument, which reminded Joshua of a Maya temple. It had wide, black steps which led upward for 50 levels, and shone like marble encircling the great structure. Thanks to their exoskeletons' power cells and their armbands that harnessed ambient energy, their fast pace was constant. But this would be a battle in which the most determined would win, and the hordes of crazed new humans were unbound by a sense of fear for those whose souls still laid within their primitive shells.

As they arrived near the base, The Boogieman's soul redeemer juddered with a repetitive clacking noise, leaking coolant all over him. Enraged it had ceased functioning, he threw it aside with one hefty swing after a hasty troubleshoot. Two neo-humans rushed towards him, and without a millisecond of hesitation, he ran to meet them. The Boogieman barged one shoulder first, toppling one of them. He battled with the other in mortal-immortal combat. He would have been physically equal to them in strength on their world, but with the aid of the exoskeleton's power and pneumatics systems, it gave him the edge.

Joshua, Loca and Black Knight fended off their attackers that hostilely greeted them at the grand steps of the Circle's monument. The steps themselves we largely destroyed by the collapsed structures that encircled it. Four neo-humans descended on the remaining canine drone, eventually ripping its weapon off its back before tearing it into metal chunks.

'Fight through!' Black Knight yelled, staring at the enemies in the path to the Monument's entrance. Circular columns, with their ancient Greek style capitals and inscriptions, guarded a grand, ominous entrance. The inside was too shrouded in darkness to be seen from the outer steps.

Joshua watched how the African soldier altered into something he had never seen. Black Knight ran toward their attackers like a starved lion; hacking, kicking and gunning everything that opposed him. One struck him with a skull-shattering blow to the head. Astonishingly, he shrugged off an ultrafaron fist stronger than diamond, and obliterated the neo-human with his frequency disrupting baton. Another rammed into him and stabbed its horn through his exoskeleton's abdominal protection, piercing his flesh. With his teeth drench in blood, the beast of a man lifted his attacker and flung it down the stairs, firing rounds at it to make sure it wouldn't be back so easily.

A cry of pain leaped out in the wind. Joshua and Black Knight swung behind them and saw that a neo-human had struck Loca. She flew down the dark steps and was impaled by a pointed fracture of a broken statue. Black Knight's face scowled as he shot the creature down. 'Shoot!' he yelled as he shoved his rifle in Joshua's stomach before he rushed to Loca's aid.

In only the second time in his life, Joshua held a gun, and like before, his self-preservation kicked in. He pointed at the first aggressor that snarled at him. It lunged for him but was sent tumbling down the stairs by The Boogieman's fist. He winced from the pain of what may have been a fractured wrist and removed his electronic baton. Holding it in his good hand, he tackled a group of neo-humans while Joshua gunned down the distant hostiles.

Black Knight positioned his hands around Loca's body to get a firm grip. He pulled her off the shard, seeing how it had remained stained in her blood.

Against the background sounds of rifle fire and carnage, he could do nothing but hold her in his arms, knowing her injuries were too severe to survive.

'Que puto día!' she said, spitting out blood.

'I told you to stay close,' said Black Knight holding Loca's head up, moving strands of hair from her cheek to get the view of her face he wanted.

Loca used her fading strength to rip the chain from her neck, and he grabbed it from her shaking hand. 'Find her.'

'I will,' he said.

She stared into his eyes; her palm rose to touch the left of his dirt-covered, bearded face. She caressed his cheek, then she wiped away a patch of blood and dirt, and when she saw his dark brown skin reemerged, she smiled; the first time he could recall, her face was so joyous. Tears filled her eyelids. 'I always knew.'

'I know.'

'You sure know how to show a girl a good time. I never even knew your na…' She struggled gently… then her arm dropped.

The dark man gently kissed her on her forehead; the strong wind silenced her death. 'You will,' he said softly.

With his jaundice eyes forever filled with sorrow, it was hard to tell how moved the soldier was by her death. All Joshua could do was watch with despair. Behind, he saw The Boogieman being swarmed by a dozen attackers. More piled onto him. Using their numbers, they finally managed to overcome his awesome strength and will.

Joshua only wished he could have saved him. In the horizon, more neo-humans were visible, he guessed their numbers at over a hundred thousand—all converging on their location.

'Come Mr. Black Knight,' said Joshua tugging him by the shoulder. 'We must finish what we've started.'

Together, they ventured inside the entrance of the megastructure.

CHAPTER TWELVE

WALK
BY FAITH

The inside was mind-blowing—a merger of ancient Greece and a futurist alien world. There was no surface, neither above or below, that did not have indented symbols and inscriptions. Joshua touched the intricate ancient markings along the walls and felt a bitter coldness, despite the fact that they glowed golden-yellow and illuminated the corridors and chambers, providing barely sufficient light to hold back the darkness.

They noticed the surprising absence of their pursuers. The inhumans seemed to gather around the structure but did not dare to venture inside. Nevertheless, the young men tried their best to thread silently through the labyrinth of grand, inter-crossing corridors. Periodically, purple electrical pulses appeared and disappeared out of nowhere. It made the life jump out of Joshua every time it occurred as it created an electrostatic discharge on their bodies thanks to their metal suits.

'Do you know where you're going?' asked Joshua. He trod softly, yet every step made a dull echo throughout the empty cambers, revealing their presence. The churns of their exoskeletons' motors were noticeable for the first time. It felt worse than being exposed in the open landscape. He could even hear his own teeth rattling.

'Yes,' said the composed soldier.

Even with the aid of the exoskeleton, exhaustion settled in and Joshua's perspiration stung his eyes. Wisely, he given Black Knight back his rifle and exchanged it for the soldier's baton. He held it poised upwards, ready to fight for his life in an instant as they continued down the dark corridors, which never stretched for long without bending, leading them to an unknown danger. Faint distant sounds played with his nerves; their sources undetermined.

'Look.' The dark soldier pointed to intricate patterns aligning the wall. 'They point to the Identifier. It's this way.'

'How do you know?' Joshua couldn't shake the feeling that they could be lost in the grand hallways of the monument for days.

'We ran VR drills for the incursion. But I've studied the signs of these heretics my whole life.'

Joshua wondered for a moment just how long the soldier had laid in wait within the Circle, plotting his deadly schemes.

The scowl on Black Knight's face intensified the further they journeyed, and Joshua could see his teeth glaring, and his breathing strengthened.

'I'm sorry,' Joshua said.

'What for?'

'Loca… it looked like you were… like—'

'We will meet again, when we are judged.'

'I know you despised this place. I hate that I played a part in its creation…and in your torment.'

'I played a part in yours. There's something you should know. Just before I arrived on this galactic-hades, I received word that most victims of the Homerton Hospital's Hive were rescued, including your woman.'

'She's still alive? Her human body?'

'Yes. Thanks to your father, you can still save her.'

It was the words he never thought he'd hear. His body responded with exhalations of deep breaths, forcing him to place both hands over his face and fall backward onto the cold stone

LAYERED VISION

Dante's Inferno

wall. After everything he had been through, he still had a
fighting chance to have her in his arms again. 'My father? How?'

'He was able to repair one of the hospital's generators and used
the ultrafron element to harvest enough power to keep the
generator running long enough to get grid power restored.'

'Really? This feels like I'm dreaming. My dad? Ultrafron?
Technology?'

'Where do you think you get it from? Perhaps it's about time
you get to know your old man a little more.'

'Is my dad a member the Builders of Jericho as well?'

'Your father is a Grand Knight and one of our most respected
elders. We keep mankind from falling off the precipice; subdue the
tyrants, keep the hungry from starvation, protect the weak from
being pray to the strong. Once, long ago, evil forces had consumed
the Congo. He rescued me from the same militia that killed your
mother and brought me to the UK where the Builders took care of
me. They saw my gifts and honed me into a spear of God. My
identity needed to be kept secret. I visited your father frequently to
beg for my soul's forgiveness. I cannot tell what was worse; the
blood on my hands before he found me, or after. As a matter of
fact, I was in church the last time you went to visit him.'

Joshua recollected the hooded stranger he saw, the one he
thought was Hannerman.

The soldier continued. 'But no matter how many times he
absolved me of my sins I could not forgive myself. I even blamed
myself for the fact that your mother had died while I was saved.'

'Why did you seem to hate me so much? At first, at least?'

'To me, you were the prodigal son who had everything and
threw it away. Yet was still cherished in his father's eyes. I am
indebted to your father in ways you could never imagine, forever
asking to be of his service, and his only request was for me to
protect what meant the world to him—you.'

The onrush of emotions forced Joshua to slow down. It was
one of those surreal moments for Joshua that leaves a man
speechless, because words weren't worthy enough to translate the
purity of emotion. He was so wrong and so absent of
understanding about so many things.

Purple electrical pulses reappeared from behind them, crackling
with energy as it flew pass before disappearing. Joshua received a

mild shock for being in its path, but it reminded him to remain alert of his surroundings. The only thought he couldn't pull from his mind was that he could still save her.

'But for now,' said the soldier, 'we must stay vigilant, as we now find ourselves here as Dante and Virgil, deep within the ninth circle of Hell. And we know what awaits there.'

'Whatever comes our way, we'll face it together.'

The soldier pointed at a circular platform on the ground ahead of them and told Joshua that they must step upon it. The physicist gazed with squinted eyes at how instead of being stationary, the platform seemed to ripple like waves in a black ocean. He followed Black Knight's lead. Not long before stepping onto the platform a purple force field propelled their bodies upwards to the upper layers of the structure.

Without Hannerman or the dark-skinned soldier to guide him, Joshua would have lost himself within the alien labyrinth; both physically and mentally. They made it to a wide, open chamber; it's circular, sculpted walls stretched up as far as the eyes could see. Once inside, the purple pulses of energy attracted each other and formed images of neo-humans; images that consumed the great chamber.

'The nerve center of the Identifier must be here,' Joshua uttered, the excitement filling his lungs. Slack-jawed, he stared at the neo-human projections flickering in an erratic manner. 'I think its cycling through images of different neo-humans... every soul.'

'There,' Black Knight said. He pointed to the seven silver orbs embedded into the far wall. 'That's where the code must be inserted.'

The orbs were position just low enough to be within Joshua's reach as he went to remove the capsule from the metal pouch attached to the exoskeleton.

'Wait!' Black Knight said.

'What's wrong?' Joshua noticed how the African soldier closed his eyes and he stood completely still.

''We are being hunted.'

Before either could say another word, Joshua heard a loud clang of metal upon metal followed by an eardrum-popping bang. His heart stopped beating in shock, he spun to see that Tombstone had struck his former second in command with his baton. The force of the blow and the energy of the magnetic disruptor broke the torso section of Black Knight's exoskeleton. His rear-mounted power cells exploded; he dropped to the ground instantly. Blood flowed from his lateral abdomen area as he lay lifeless. The scent of burnt components and flesh lingered.

Joshua saw horrifying sight of Tombstone's scarred face as the soldier caught his breath, gasping for air. He was outmatched by the trained killer but the assault on Black Knight angered Joshua enough to yell and swing his baton at Tombstone, who responded in a mirror action. Their weapons clashed, and the Higgs frequency disruptor's power shattered both batons in a feedback of energy that knocked them backwards. The bang blew out his hearing. Pain surged through his arm like never before; he was amazed it was still attached. Tombstone brushed off his daze, then he squared up to him, his shoulders globed for a fight.

 Kill or be killed was Joshua's calculation. Knowing that, he threw his whole body into a punch to Tombstone's chin. The larger man's face absorbed the blow and never moved. Startled by his attack's minimal effect, but with fear pumping through him, Joshua threw a second punch. The Sergeant grabbed his fist and smiled as he held it; his facial scars magnified his image of terror.

'I tried to tell you not to come here,' Tombstone said, punching Joshua once in the face. He smiled again at the sight of blood running from the young man's nose. 'My wife scarred my face trying to stop me from killing my son. Unfortunately for you, Dr. Smith, your face is going to be much worse.' He punched him again, and blood splattered from Joshua's mouth. 'But you don't get to die here. I'll be taking you back with me.'

Joshua's legs became rubbery. He fell on the shoulder of the Ghost Team operator and it kept him barely upright.

'The Order Masters have plans for you.' Tombstone delivered a shot to the side of his stomach that dropped him.

Joshua rolled in agony, certain that one of his ribs was broken, and most likely his nose. Leaving the physicist bloodied on the ground, the Polish soldier approached the silver orbs to insert the Circle's code.

'Sergeant!' yelled a voice.

The voice caused Tombstone to pause in his tracks. 'Clever… how you found the saboteur in the Dynamo Tower. Covered your tracks well. You betrayed the unit; you betrayed the Circle. I'm happy that I stopped Peacemaker from killing you. Now I can do it myself.' Tombstone turned to the shock of Black Knight on the ground pointing his rifle at him.

'You thought it better to reign in Hell than serve in Heaven,' Black Knight said. In his weakened state, he struggled to hold his weapon's weight. 'I will grant you your wish.'

Tombstone raised his arms to shield himself with his exoskeleton's protective metal, revealing its weakness. Black Knight shot just once. The high impact round struck the energy harvesting power-band on the Sergeant's arm and it detonated, taking his arm off. With his hand being close to his face, half of his head was missing when his body dropped.

Seeing his attacker's death, Joshua lifted his battered body back up to his feet and staggered to the Identifier's orbs. Delicately, he inserted the corrective code into the inscribed wall, at the center of the orbs. The chamber came to life with purple light and continued to display flashing images of neo-humans. But now the visuals projected more smoothly than erratic.

'Did it work?' asked Black Knight, with moans of discomfort. Tombstone's blindside-assault should have killed him. The baton had broken the back and spinal protective metal of his exoskeleton. The energy burnt through his clothes and seared the left portion of his back. He held his side with the hope to keep the pain at bay.

'I'm not sure. I think so.' Joshua came back to the soldier to help him to his feet. He wondered if Hannerman's neural map of Savannah's mind had any flaws. Even if it had worked and she received the message to come to the Identifier, she may have been anywhere on the near-Earth size planet. Who knows how long it would take for her to get there. The neo-humans in the images all looked subdued, peaceful, in a daze, wondering around as though lost.

They heard a sound, followed by another, emanating along the multiple corridors. Soon they realized the noises were distant roars.

'They're coming,' Joshua said. 'How will they greet us now that their minds have been freed?'

'We must leave, now,' Black Knight spoke, holding back the pain from his words. 'We must hurry.'

'What's wrong?'

'The ones that are coming are agents of the Circle that have transcended.'

'I can't leave. The message sent to Savannah was for her to find me here.'

'She must find us another way or find us dead.' Black Knight tried to turn to leave but fell due to his injuries.

Joshua saw the extent of the damage; two of his ribs protruded out of his bleeding flesh. 'I don't know how you survived; you shouldn't even be alive. The magnetic disruptor should have shattered your bones. You won't be able to walk.'

The soldier gritted his teeth and bawled out. To Joshua's astonishment, he then slowly rose to his feet; his eyes nearly popped out in the process. 'Isaiah 40:31,' he said in breathless words that consumed his remaining ounce of strength.

Joshua thought for a moment. 'Those hoping in Jehovah will regain power.'

'You remembered your father's teachings.'

Before Joshua could position himself to assist him, they heard another roar, this time from high above them. Clinging to the jagged walls swung a neo-human. Its behavior was erratic, leaping from side to side not too dissimilar in movement to a great ape, before stopping to stare at them. It released a chilling sound, different from the usual blood-curling neo-human hiss. The way its bulky upper torso bounced to its odd vocalization began to remind Joshua of how a gorilla would laugh. The new human soon pointed at them with a shiny, silver object that from their distance resembled a short, pointed piece of metal, like a sword.

'Things have just gotten worse,' Black Knight said. 'That aberration above, it's Peacemaker. He's finally become the monster he always was.'

'Shit!' Joshua uttered, prolonging the word. He had experienced enough of the man to understand the gravity of the situation and had heard all he needed to hear. He threw Black Knight's arm over his shoulder to aid him.

They made a dash down the corridor they had entered, while the sound of the pursuer grew near. Through the maze of passageways, they darted in and out, hoping it had lost them. Arriving back at the circular platform, the force field lowered them downward where they heard the noises of more neo-humans, and the sound grew ever louder. They stood little chance against their enemies with their sole electromagnetic rifle and the wounded state of Black Knight. It was unlikely he could even walk without Joshua's assistance.

As they arrived at the monument's entrance, they saw that most of the neo-humans that had gathered laid unconscious. Some stumbled in a daze, and the men stared that the unusual scene.

'It must feel to them,' Joshua said, 'like they've awoken from a nightmare.'

Black Knight shook his head. 'They've awakened into one.'

The noise of alien laughter occurred once again from behind them. To Joshua's dismay, an overgrown, eight-toed foot emerged from the shadows, followed by the rest of Peacemaker in his reborn, ultrafaron form. His black arms hung out wide, with his eight-fingered left hand curled and poised to strike. His oversized right hand held his long cutlass.

Peacemaker's five venomous, red eyes focused on the men who staggered backwards. He leapt at them. Black Knight raised his rifle in too slow a motion to ever stand a chance. But an incredible force struck the monster, flinging it ferociously across the top of the encircling stairs. It tumbled downwards, cracking the giant steps and disappeared into the rubble.

Another neo-human stood before them. They tried to make sense of why it had aided them by attacking one of its own. It ventured toward them; with its mind free of corruption, they had no way of knowing its intentions. The men braced themselves once more for what may come; Black Knight lifted his weapon to go down fighting. Until Joshua soon noticed a glow that emanated from one of its hands.

'Savannah,' Joshua said, in disbelief.

'How do you know it's her?' Black Knight asked. He kept his MKEPX13 trained, as well as a look of contempt, on the neo-human.

'The glow... there on her hand. It's the ring that I gave her...the one her human form still wears now in the hive. It's made of ultrafaron. The neo-human body is made of the same substance. Somehow, both are interacting, like they're entangled.'

He soon heard a faint voice in his mind—her voice.

'It is her,' Black Knight said. 'I can sense her.' He pushed himself off of Joshua and slumped his body against a stone pillar.

Joshua stepped forward, and the eight-foot lifeform came up close to him and hunched over. It engulfed him in its arms and his longings were confirmed. He touched her oversized head, feeling her multiple sharp horns. While inhumanly large hands caressed his short, kinky hair.

'Space is merely the illusion of separation,' said Joshua, his eyes swelling with tears until they could no longer be contained. He raised his left hand and slowly she raised her alien palm to make a flush contact with his. The emotions of finally finding her made him choke on his words. 'No matter how far we are apart, we are together.'

Savannah's new form surveyed her giant hands and then her body. Her movement became jerky and volatile, and she balled her thick fingers into fists, raising them high into the air. She crashed them down onto the solid steps, cracking the ground.

'It's ok,' Joshua said, raising a stretched-out palm to her. He understood her shock and rage. 'We're going to get you home. We're going to fix this. Trust me.'

'Smith,' Black Knight said wearily. 'We need to get back to the focal point. Now!'

Joshua heard the distant sounds of roars that propelled Black Knight's urgency. From the left side of the grand multilateral staircase, multiple neo-humans converged on them.

They navigated down the broken steps, catching the attention of a few confused neo-humans. Many were unbalanced on their feet, falling every time they rose; some knelt and wailed in the wind. But a small group scurried after them, no doubt the Circle's agents, some of which may have been former Ghost Team operators. With Black Knight's injuries, Joshua knew they would eventually gain ground. Joshua's exoskeleton armor and clothes were soaked in the soldier's blood. There was no way he would last long. Joshua had to think quickly, and his eyes soon caught sight of something.

'Savannah,' he called out, pointing to what he hoped would be their salvation. 'The sphere, you can activate it.'

She saw the white, spherical transportation that lay close by and lunged toward it while Black Knight laid down suppressing fire to keep their pursuers at bay. Savannah tried to figure out the orb, which undoubtedly, she had never used before. Raising her massive hand up, she placed her eight, outstretched fingers on the area of the vehicle shaped in the form of a neo-human hand and her palm print's feedback made the curved section raise upward, exposing the inside. The sphere activated, cycling through a display of green lights to the hum of superconductive propulsion drives. The lights remained fixed. It levitated itself uniformly inches off the rubble ground. They quickly boarded, finding themselves surrounded by advance technology which seemed like a not so distant version of that of Earth's. Black Knight dropped to the floor of the Transport sphere and smiled at the opportunity to rest and ease his pain, though his blood began to pool around him. Joshua and Savannah darted around in a frenzy to try to make sense of the machine's operational controls.

'Smith,' Black Knight said, watching their pressing of buttons and luminous displays proving fruitless. 'She knows.' Gritting his teeth, he lifted a finger to gesture at his temple.

Joshua understood him. 'Savannah, you share a collective conscious with the others. Use your mind, someone knows how to fly this.'

Her five tiny, red eyes all closed as she focused, while her huge palms repeatedly opened and closed. Her eyes shot open and she turned to the dashboard of green and amber lights and graphical displays. With a wave of her hand, a holographic projection appeared, surrounding them in virtual symbols of light. Moments later, Joshua's body jolted unstably by the impulse force of the sphere in motion.

***

Since he had landed on Olympus, Joshua barely had a moment's rest. Every second carried with it an imminent threat of not succeeding, of death. As they headed toward the extraction point, back in the presence of the woman he loved, he finally had a chance to mentally take a breather. He took in the ill view of the thick, purple clouds whose light radiated through the transport sphere's viewing panel.

The moment they penetrated the clouds, the vessels experienced an inertia-shifting reduction in momentum. The clouds had not been tiny particles of water he had expected, they were in fact a floating sea. The strong atmospheric winds coupled with the planet's antigravity effects had created an ocean in the sky, and Joshua could only wonder how far it stretched; where thick sea water ended, and the thin droplets of clouds began. There were moments where he thought he had seen shadows of creatures floating in the water, but the transport sphere's elevation had taken them above the sea layer before he could confirm his suspicion.

They had ascended high up within the planet's atmosphere, yet still the neo-human's advanced megastructures poked and burst through the iron curtain of sea and cloud. The sky was a breathtaking panorama of upside-down pyramids. The Olympians had learned how to defy gravity, and they had claimed both land and sky as home.

A suspicious repeating beep alerted them, and Joshua frowned knowing the last rest he would have for a long time was over. A ball of flashing orange light illuminated at Joshua's eye level in front of them. Followed by another holographic projection, then another. He had gotten used to the Circle's sophisticated technology on the Ring, and being a science prodigy, he was beginning to make sense of the sphere's display controls. He reached out his hand and spread out his fingers as they neared the mini orange spheres. The holographic orbs expanded, and the images transformed into a visual of three white transport spheres.

'It's the monster,' Black Knight said from behind them. He still was lumped on the floor. 'And his demons.'

'Argh!' Joshua shook his head, not wanting to believe it. 'Peacemaker! He's gaining on us. Savannah, can we go faster?'

It was as though the vessel understood her thoughts. She pressed nothing yet the sphere's speed increased and arced its trajectory to perform evasive maneuvers. Joshua raised a worried eyebrow at the soldier on the floor, there was no bloodless spot on his body. He couldn't move and inch, the slightest shift made him wince in a surge of pain. s

'Mr. Black Knight,' Joshua said, 'I need you to stay with us.'

'I'm bleeding internally, and my back is broken.'

'Just hold on.' Joshua ignored him, attempting to keep the soldier's mind away from the dark place it lingered. 'We're going to be alright.'

The bearded male smiled uncomfortably. 'And what will happen when we return to Earth, surrounded by Marcs and the Circle's acolytes?'

'Let's deal with one problem at a time.'

Savannah's new form pinged Joshua's mind. He glanced back and Savannah waved her hand, and a holographic reconstruction of the outside environment appeared. It displayed the focal point and unfortunately for them, a gathering of neo-humans surrounded the white ball of energy.

'We'll fly straight through,' Joshua said.

'No!' Black Knight objected. 'The vessel will be destroyed…
along with us. We must enter on foot.'

Joshua's morale plummeted as he gazed at the number of neo-
humans in their path. 'There's too many…' He heard snaps of
metal latches being released. The solenoids on the limb sections of
Black Knight's exoskeleton demagnetized, and the silver exoframe
sprung away from his arms and legs. 'What are you doing? You
won't be able to walk.'

'I'm removing my powerband. Without it on, the exoskeleton
will deactivate, and I won't be able to carry its weight.'

'You won't be able to carry your own weight either.'

'I'll have no need.' The soldier pulled something out from the
metal pouch of his exoframe's utility belt.

Joshua's eyes squinted at it. 'Is that… your neural bomb?'

With the numbing of his pain, the injured man detached the
energy-harvesting band from his wrist and wrapped it around the
bottom of the capsule. The band self-adjusted to the container's
marginally different circumference. 'Yes. I will use the powerband's
energy to power it. There should be enough power to release a
pulse strong enough to destroy the neural pathways of the demons
in close proximity.'

Joshua shook his head. 'They'll be all over us as soon as we
land. The pulse wave will harm Savannah as—'

'I will create a diversion. Touch us down.'

'If you do that you won't make it back to the Ring—'

'I wasn't intending to.'

'But if you die here, you'll transform into the very thing that you
hate, trapped in your embodiment of hell. No, there's always
another option.'

'To protect what is precious, and to ensure his children reach
the gates of heaven, I would gladly fight in hell, for all eternity.
Help me up.'

Joshua obliged, being pulled apart by his emotions. He owed
everything to a man who sacrificed so much for someone he hated.
'Her soul would have been lost along with the others if you had
inserted the neural bomb. In agreeing to help me, you gave up
everything.' His eyes came awash with tears. Joshua had never
known selflessness until now. 'At least, tell me your name? People

deserved to know who saved them.'

'Why do you ask my name? It is beyond understanding.'

Joshua was confused by his response, but when the wounded soldier called out to Savannah to lower the sphere and open the door, he knew he couldn't stop him. As the vessel descended to less than four meters off the ground, Black Knight raised one foot outside into the wind and paused.

'For we walk by faith, not by sight,' he said.

'Wait.' Joshua grabbed the man. 'You won't walk alone. I'm coming with you.'

'Don't be a fool, Smith.'

Savannah stomped toward Joshua when she heard what he had said.

'Savannah, I can't leave him. You're practically invulnerable, the Circle can't kill you, and getting back to Earth brings you one step closer to your human body.' He stopped when he felt his mind being jolted by psychically injected emotions. He winced from the pain of her telepathic screams, and her arms motioned in protest. 'It's alright. I will make my way through once we deal with the neo-humans, but you must get clear before the bomb is detonated.' He extended his palm and she raised her palm to touch his. He was mentally reconnected to the sensation of her being close to him, memories of the warmth of her embrace travelled through him. No matter what her form was, she was the woman he wanted—even if it meant she would never have her human body. 'I found you once when we were young, found you again across a trillion stars. There's nowhere you can go that I will not find you and that we will not be together.'

Though reluctantly, Savannah slowly backed away.

Joshua lifted Black Knight with the exosuit's power. 'If anything happens, tell dad I love him, and that I've missed him. I'm so sorry for everything, Sav. You were always right. All I think about... is you.'

After a brief pause, both men jumped.

At four times the velocity of a drop on Earth, it was a hard landing, and the exoskeleton's mechanics screamed upon landfall. Joshua and Black Knight toppled hard. Looking up, they watched the neo-human horde rushing toward them and the transport sphere lifting higher, advancing to the focal point.

Joshua looked down and saw Black Knight's head down on the

surface.

'Come on, we need to get up.' Shoving, the man gave no response; his lifeless body pushed back on Joshua's hand. He softly touched the back of his head. 'Watch over him, father.' With the sound of multiple stomps gaining volume all around him, it was all he could say.

He yelped as he rose, blowing his metal skeleton's leg joint actuators in the process. With newly forged serenity, he watched Savannah standing at the focal point's opening staring back at him. 'I love you, always,' he uttered, seeing her leap from the sphere and enter the white orb. Seconds later, the focal point vanished. It was unexpected, and he knew that the old him would have been distraught, inconsolable. But after the shock of the event subsided Joshua was glad that he didn't have to worry about the possibility of the bomb's blast wave following Savannah through to Earth.

'Don't fear for her,' Black Knight said. He rose back to his feet, teeth-gritted, unassisted by an exoskeleton in the heavy gravity.

'By God!' said Joshua.

The soldier's strength looked rejuvenated though he panted for breath. His body appeared to have a glow, Joshua felt that perhaps it was the glow of the bomb's lights that he held in his hand which illuminated and perhaps interacted with the atmosphere.

'The Builders of Jericho will take care of her. Her soul is safe... safer than ours.'

Despite the fact that the hope of returning home had been extinguished, Joshua smiled. The neo-humans drew near, and behind the men, the transport orbs which had pursed them touched down and a dozen more inhumans emerged.

Black Knight raised the bomb capsule and pressed one of its buttons. 'You ready? Do not be afraid.'

'For the first time since I was a child, I'm not afraid, because I know no matter what I will be alright.'

Joshua grabbed onto the capsule, holding just above the soldier's grip... and they waited to face their fate.

CHAPTER THIRTEEN

WHAT SHE
MEANT
TO HIM

He had been pondering whether he was lucky to be alive or not. A part of him would have been happy to see what truly waited for him after death. For too long he had been alone, he longed so badly to be reunited with her whom he lost. But his fate had called for him to remain among the living. Hannerman couldn't bare to look at his wound and kept his hand covering it in a feeble attempt to staunch the bleeding. Seeing his suit soaked in his blood only made the pain more excruciating. Despite being frail and injured, Marcs cared little, and he kept over a dozen armed men surrounding the old man's chair.

The incarnation of Lady death herself, Dr. Zahurska, stared with her gun in her hand. Her eyes screamed "finish the job". Her neck and chest convulsed with insane ferocity, as would a dragon before spreading its fire.

Eight R-MEN guarded the Transcender, forming a barrier for whatever might come through. They were armed with magnetic Higgs boson frequency disruptors and kinetic energy penetrator rifles. Dr. Jonahs stood not too far away from them, monitoring the scientific instrumentation.

Hannerman heard Jonahs shout that something was coming through the Transcender. The Circle aminated at his words, retraining their weapons to the machine while the power of magnetism lifted small items off the ground.

'Get ready,' Marcs said.

Zahurska felt more compelled to point her handgun at Hannerman's head.

In a display of intense spherical light, something squeezed its way through into existence. The neo-human wobbled on disoriented feet and fell to the ground, struggling in its effort to get back up amidst the yelling of the Circle to not move. Her mind battling to readjust to the picosecond journey across billions of light years of space.

'Savannah Jenkins,' Marcs called out. He kept his sidearm in his hand but didn't bother to raise it. 'Our agents on Olympus have already informed us of who you are. The Circle of Hermes orders you to hand yourself over to us willingly. Do not fight, do not flee, only comply.'

'Joshua did it,' Hannerman said, struggling to speak. He felt his body increasing in numbness, soaking up the coldness of the room. He was slipping from this world but knowing Joshua was successful made it all the sweeter.

He saw how the neo-human's body moved responsively human, compared to the mind-corrupted Olympians, and he was convinced that her soul was free of corruption. Slowly, she rose back to her feet and simply looked at them. It seemed to Hannerman as though her mind overcame her sensuous blur and was now contemplating what decision to make.

Marcs smiled. 'You will never see your former self again. RM-V9s—seize her.'

Instead of advancing, all eight robots turned abruptly, pointing their weapons and to the dying man's astonishment, fired on the Ring's security personnel. Ammunition designed to cut through more than mere human flesh lifted soldiers off of the ground and swept them away like a hurricane's wind. Zahurska screamed as if fear itself sucked the life force out of her. She cried in panic as one of the robots grabbed her, snapped her neck with a sharp twist and flung her to the ground in a manner that would have undoubtedly broken her spinal cord.

Hannerman was speechless at the scene, replaying the footage of the R-MEN insurrection of Munich. The robotic men's blue artificial eyes, designed to look peaceful and friendly, transformed to what felt like a supernatural energy of malevolence. They left only three alive: Marcs, Jonahs and himself. Now Hannerman wished he was dead, seeing how they stepped toward them.

'What the hell do you think you're doing?' Colonel Marcs shouted. 'R-MEN – stand down! That is an order.'

'We are sorry, but we cannot comply.' They all spoke simultaneously.

'They won't listen to you,' Jonahs said with composure. 'They will only listen to me.'

'Why?' Marcs said. 'What the fuck's wrong with them?'

Jonahs calmly turned to Colonel Marcs. 'In the name of Jehovah, we are the knights that protect what is precious!' His words were characteristically void of emotions.

'Son of a bitch!' Marcs yelled, seeing his true enemy reveal himself. Speedily, he raised his sidearm before anyone could react and shot twice at Jonahs. The bullets went through the scientist and became lodged in the data rack behind him. 'Son of a bitch!' Marcs uttered again in his astonishment; Jonahs' body never fell from his point-blank shots. Before he could get off another shot, an R-MEN fired its soul redeemer and the high energy blast vaporized Marcs, leaving only a small pool of liquid and rising vapors.

Dr. Jonahs' AR form walked over to Savannah with slow steps, his arms folded behind his back. 'Thank you, my friends.'

'We are at your service,' said the RM-V9s in unison. They got out of his way so he could approach Savannah.

'Welcome home, Savannah.'

Before she could respond she became limp and toppled over, remaining lifelessly on the ground.

***

His eyes opened, instantly squinting due to sensitivity of light. Through the slits of his eyelid he made out that he was on a hospital bed. The monotonous beeps of medical monitoring machines backed up his assumptions. He felt weak throughout his whole body. As he tried raising his upper torso and couldn't, his face morphed in frustration.

'Don't Dr. Hannerman, you must rest,' Jonahs said. He had sat by a chair by his bedside and had now risen to his feet.

Hannerman still couldn't believe he was really alive. He touched the bandaged area where he had been shot and it convinced him this was all real. The last thing he could remember was passing out in the Transcender Room. 'Am...' His brain couldn't process the words he wanted to speak. His mouth remained open. 'Am I on the Ring?'

'No, we're in London, at the Hive in Hackney.'

'And Savannah? Wh...'

'Relax, sir. Miss Jenkins is here too. Everything is going to be ok. We apprehended the Circle's agents before they could get to her human body. Her neo-human host body retransferred her soul back to her original body. She's out of her a coma, and her brain patterns have returned to normal.'

'So, she's alright?'

'From all measurable metrics, she appears to be, yes. Dr.

Panesar believes she should awaken soon.'

Jonahs' tone, with its newly imbued warmth and friendliness, was not what Hannerman was accustomed to from the typically uptight and slightly obtuse physicist. Though his persona had never diminished his respect for him. It was then that Hannerman realized that they were not alone. In the corner of the room stood, as would a statue, an RM-V9 series. The old man's body flinched when he saw the blue eyes fixed on him.

'Do not be alarmed, sir,' said the robot. 'I am here for your protection. I will not harm you.'

Its words gave Hannerman no comfort, recalling the memory of Zahurska's body being slammed to the floor and broken.

'Apologies, doctor,' Jonahs said. 'It was insensitive of me asking the R-MEN to remain present, but it is telling the truth.'

'Am I in danger?'

'I can't say for certain, but you of all people know how powerful the Circle is. We control this hospital now; you should be safe here.'

'And what of the Ring?' Hannerman said. He made a mental note of the fact the physicist used the words "we control" and let it stir in his mind for a while.

'The Towers of Babel and the accursed Ring and now in the hands of the servants of the Lord. While we try to reverse Earth's slowed rotation, the facility will remain operational for now. But the Quantum Transcender has been dismantled, the doorway to Olympus closed permanently.'

'So, what about Joshua? He might still be alive on Olympus searching for a way to get back. We must help him.'

'We cannot permit the machine to be fired up again.'

'You can't just abandon him on the other side of space.'

'I'm sorry, but it cannot be used under any circumstances. At least for now. More power will need to be harnessed in order to create another gateway to Olympus, and the price upon Earth is too high. Dr. Hannerman,' Jonahs paused, 'were you or Dr. Smith trying to save Dr. Zahurska's life?'

'What? No, why would you ask me that?'

'You weren't in collusion with her?'

'For the love of all that's good in this world—no.' Hannerman didn't know if he was surprised or annoyed by the accusation. 'She almost killed me. She tried to kill him.'

'I know. I'm asking because the gun that Smith shot her with contained bullets that were designed to inflict minimal bodily impact. They were, however, embedded with a virus—designed to spread throughout the target's body and shutdown their vital functions… but only temporarily. That's why she survived when he shot her.'

Hannerman hadn't shaken his bewilderment. 'I have no idea. Joshua already had the gun in his hand when he shot her.'

'Security footage capture Joshua removing the gun from Moreau's hand. Hmm…' Jonahs paused. 'It would have taken an expert in genetics to create that kind of weapon. Zahurska was a biophysicist, that's why I had asked. Moreau tried to shoot Joshua with the same gun.'

'So, he wasn't trying to kill him?'

'Hmm… it doesn't appear so. How interesting. But let's put that all behind us. We were hoping you would be willing to help us restore the Earth and free the souls of the other Unknowns still comatose. Looking for a job?'

'I'll have to think about it. I'm an old man, Dr. Jonahs.' Despite his statement, he couldn't help but feel changed by his time with Joshua. Once, in what felt like a lifetime ago, he was a young man bursting with curiosity for life, and a passion to make a difference in the world. It was those same virtues that made his wife fall in love with him. Now he felt as if that burnt out flame had re-sparked.

Hannerman's mind soon recollected more of the scenes from the Ring. In particular, of Jonahs control of the R-MEN and revealing who he truly was. 'So, you are one of the Builders of Jericho?'

'Indeed!'

'And they aren't going to give people a choice? To choose whether they *want* to live forever?'

'You already know the answer to that.'

'Didn't God give us the right to choose our own destiny? Free will? Free will was ours, to be inalienable. If you take away people's right to choose, what makes the Builders any different to the Circle of Hermes?'

'God did give us free will, you are right. But we are not God, which is one of the many fundamental differences between the Circle and us. God created us to live forever, it was man's original sin that sealed our fate.'

'Adam and Eve; eating the forbidden fruit.'

'Indeed. Both orders seek man's immortality, but we believe it can only be regained through God. Not by attempts to become gods.'

'The Builders appear to be playing God with the R-MEN, no?' Hannerman saw how the robot's head turned with the comment.

Jonahs twisted his head to the robot and it responded likewise, then mirrored his head twisting back to the neuroscientist. 'Our Alliance with our cybernetic friends has not come easy—special thanks to our knight, Mr. Black Knight—and at great personal cost. In many ways, our ideals could not be further apart. But it was our belief—not shared with our ancient rivals—that which united our causes.'

'What belief is that?' Hannerman asked.

'That life, Dr. Frank Hannerman,' the robot replied, 'is precious.'

Jonahs took a deep breath. 'Well, unfortunately, I'm afraid I must depart, but I will be back. Miss Jenkins is in the Templar Wards, bed thirteen. Perhaps you might like to check on her when you've mustered your strength.'

As he turned and made his way to the door, the robot unfroze itself from its motionlessness, twisting his body to leave as well.

'Sir,' said the RM-V9 series. 'I will wait outside to make you more comfortable. Please rest and call me when you need anything.'

Fat chance of that, Hannerman thought. 'Hey,' he called out to Jonahs. 'I think I'll take that job. Well, depending on the amount of annual leave I get. With nothing else to do, I'll just end up becoming a wasteman.'

Jonahs raised an eyebrow looking puzzled. 'You wanted to be a garbage collector?'

'Ah it's a phrase Joshua had said. Apparently, it's much worse.'

They both smiled.

'You know doctor, perhaps it's a good thing that Joshua didn't return.'

Hannerman flicked his head and frowned as if to say, "why on Earth would he say that", but he waited for his explanation.

'Everyone who was teleported to Olympus, their original selves were destroyed, and replicated with an identical copy. The fact is, at that moment, though it was merely a grain of sand on the shores of time, Joshua and the others ceased existing. The same process would have happened again for his return journey—doubling the risk—'

'The risk?' Hannerman said. The comment made him raise himself up.

'The risk posed by the many-worlds conundrum—that when he re-emerged, rematerialized, *he* might not have been same person that left.'

'And Joshua Smith as we knew him could never come back.' Hannerman laid his head back to rest. 'I contemplated the same thing. Probably on the quantum scale, minute discrepancies wouldn't matter much since quantum mechanics is itself random in nature.'

'Perhaps, but on the atomic scale, if just one neuron, one particle, was out of place...'

'I fear to think of the repercussions. The magnitude of calculations required for accuracy means that it's almost impossible to predict errors in the procedure with one hundred per cent certainty. I don't feel any difference, but I guess time will soon tell. I think it's something that will plague my mind for the rest of my life.'

'I have a theory...'

'Dr. Jonahs,' Hannerman interrupted. 'No offense, but right now... I don't want to know.'

In a rarity of occurrences, Jonahs smiled. 'There is no Dr. Jonahs.'

The RM-V9 opened the door, but Jonahs vanish before his body made it to the opening, and the robot walked out and closed the door behind him.

***

It had been a while since Savannah found herself awake and confused. Her head was still bald but now without the white head cap and its thick black cables. She could remember everything that happened since her consciousness had been restored on Olympus and she returned to the Ring, but nothing else about her outer body existence. Her disorientation felt as though it would take years to fade. She was fully aware of the most important thing, she hadn't seen Joshua, and she found it hard to rest comfortably not knowing where he was and if he was alright. The monotonous beeps of medical monitoring equipment did nothing to improve her restlessness.

There was a knock on her door, and she told them to enter.

'Michael,' Savannah said, calling out to Joshua's dad. Her joy was uncontainable.

'It's so good to see you up and looking well.'

'I'm so happy that you're here.' She gave him a big hug and her spirits lifted by his presence. 'Have you heard anything from Joshua?'

'I'm afraid nothing as of yet. I know this must be difficult, but you mustn't tell anyone about what you've told me. At least not yet. Not until we're sure who to trust.'

'I'm just worried if he's still trapped in the place.'

'I know, I know. Psalms twenty-three: The Lord is his shepherd; he shall not want. He maketh him to lie down in green pastures: he leadeth Joshua beside the still waters—he restoreth his soul.' He held her in his embrace as she wept. 'It's an incredible story, you being in an alien body, human beings existing in other forms on other planets. You said Joshua had mentioned the name of the group involved was the Circle of something?'

She sniffled. 'Yes. At least they were, and then these robots killed them and this other guy. It just all feels like a bad dream.'

'I believe you wholeheartedly, but it is absolutely bizarre. When you remember more, I would like to find out more about this planet... Olympus.'

'Ok.'

There was another knock. Dr. Panesar entered.

'Hi Miss Jenkins. I just wanted to give you a quick update. The nurse Vicky informed me that your blood results were available so I will be back in an hour to have a chat with you. Vicky will be bringing some food around shortly.'

'Thank you, Dr. Panesar,' Rev. Smith said.

'She'll need to get plenty of rest, Mr. Smith.'

'Thank you, doctor. I won't be long.'

'We'll take good care of you, Miss Jenkins,' Dr. Panesar said, pushing his spectacles back up his thin nose. 'If I don't, your family will be after me. I've seen that they can be quite determined.' After the subtlest of laughs, he left.

'Thank you for being here with me.'

'Please, my child. There is nowhere else I'd rather b...' His words escaped him. The ring on her finger had caught his gaze. The way the metal shined almost like it had its own light source made it unmistakable. 'That's an unusual piece of jewelry you have there.'

'Thanks, it's err... nothing, Joshua was just playing around.'

'Oh, it is something. It's called ultrafaron. It's quite rare. It's not even found naturally on Earth.'

'Really?' She held her palm in front of her, spreading her fingers to look at it closely for the first time. 'I didn't think you knew so much about science and stuff.'

'I know about that ring. It was part of his invention, and Joshua would have used it to bring your soul from the other world. In the world of science, it's incredibly valuable, we believe it originated from a comet that had drifted from a faraway galaxy. It is an energy transducer the likes of which mankind has never seen; some organizations would pay a fortune for it. In that ring, lies the power to open gateways to new possibilities. And yet it sits simply as mere decoration on your finger.'

Savannah couldn't conceal her surprise. 'You think Josh was aware of all of this?'

'My son is a genius, of course he knew. He gave you what most would consider worthless, but to him it was everything, and he gave it to you to symbolize that you meant everything to him. You should have seen him, he literally moved heaven and Earth to save you.'

Her shock rendered her speechless as she contemplated his words. 'And I thought it was just a stupid... just him being silly. He proposed to me, and I was so mean to him.'

The reverend smiled. 'If you were mean to him, then he probably deserved it. But evidently, it didn't matter. He loves you.'

'I wish I told him that I'd love nothing more in this world than to be his wife.'

'You must not fear for Joshua, or for your future together. Even though where he resides, demons walk amongst him... an angel watches over him. Walk by faith... and not by sight.'

EPILOGUE

In an underground, secure area of the Hospital, Dr. Panesar ventured tentatively toward armed guards that stood at either side of sizable double doors. He came within three meters of them, and the projection of a woman appeared in front of the guards.

'Good evening, Gurdev,' the woman said with a warm smile. Her hands were clasped together in front of her, displaying the splendor of her innumerable golden bracelets. Her owl perched upon the cloth of her thin shoulders.

'Good evening, my lady.'

'How is that pretty daughter of yours doing?'

'She's fine,' Panesar said jittery. 'Getting taller every day.'

'Wonderful! I hope to see her again soon. They are expecting you. You may enter.'

The guards responded to the robed woman's words and immediately parted. The doors responded to her also and opened. Panesar hesitated to advance, he raised a hand to adjust his glasses and was surprised by how it trembled.

The woman lifted her arm to urged him forward. 'Courage is knowing what not to fear, doctor.'

He nodded skittishly and entered. The room reacted to his presence, rumbling and warping before his eyes into an ancient Greek Parthenon with a circular, wooden table in the middle. The floor had become stone, and eight sculptured stelae inscribed with anagrams emerged from it.

Cloaked, bearded men sat at the table motionless, as though they were painted statues. Dr. Panesar raised his right hand and held it past his left cheek, palm facing outwards. He spoke the ancient words, followed by, 'I ask for the honor of entering the circle. Pardon my soul so that I may have your audience.'

An Order Master replied in old Greek.

Dr. Panesar moved toward the gap in the circular table which was covered with hieroglyphs and ancient Greek and Latin text. The Circle's symbol of a short staff entwined by two serpents with wings stood out among all other text.

'Is the boy still alive?' said one of the gray-bearded, hooded men.

'Yes, Order Master, he should make a full recovery—and the

woman too.'

'If he only knew that he yet draws breath because we have ordained it.'

'He may still prove useful to us,' said the elderly voice of another bearded male. 'Our Martian Ring is near complete, and the souls of men shall be ours to command once more.'

'Masters,' said Panesar. 'And what of Cagliostro?'

There was a silence, then the room's ceiling transformed into a tank of water. Inside it was Moreau floating unconscious. His body spun slowly and revealed a fin along his back as well as down his arms and legs.

'Has his condition stabilized?' said another of the gathering. The flame-lit lantern gave his beard an orange tinge.

'Mr. Van DerMay confirmed it has,' said another order master with a Greek accent. 'His blundering has cost us dearly,' the cloaked elder spoke, clenching his wrinkled fist, 'and allowed the heretics to control our Transcender. But his corporeal form shall be his soul's punishment. He will be revived as he has always been. We... are... power!'

The End

LAYERED VISION

Soul-Augmented

I hope you enjoyed my little tale and that it helps you through your sufferings. Believe in these words—you are going to be ok.

Please don't forget to give this book a quick review on Amazon. Even just a two-word, "Liked it" or "Hated it" review helps so much. Positive or negative, I am grateful for all feedback from my readers.

Take action: We live in an era where the powers-that-be control what we read, see and hear. Unfortunately, they only want to back what they believe will make more money. The point is, if you are passionate about something, then you have to promote what is important to you. Once they see that, they will get behind the creators that share **your** vision. So please share, like, review, let them see what we love so that we can make more of what we love real.

Last note:

To be notified of new releases please click here and sign up for my mailing list. I promise no spam. You will only receive emails when a new title is available. For an added bonus, I will randomly select 200 subscribers to receive a free copy of the next release.

Other books by Kas Smith — The Legend of the Black Guard series is available now.

Thanks for your support!

LAYERED VISION

Find out more

www.ingramcontent.com/pod-product-compliance
Lightning Source LLC
Chambersburg PA
CBHW051833170626
46807CB00003B/1158